THE
SKULL
IN THE
WOOD

From The Chicken House

Ghosts are a bit like lost stories – trying to catch you by surprise, looking for a way to finish. Sandra Greaves unleashes a terrible tale, which will keep you guessing deep into the night. But don't worry, that skull is probably perfectly harmless. Like the dog.

Barry Cunningham
Publisher

THE
SKULL
IN THE
WOOD

sandra Greaves

Chicken House

2 Palmer Street, Frome, Somerset BA11 1DS

For John

Text © Sandra Greaves 2013
First published in Great Britain in 2013
The Chicken House
2 Palmer Street
Frome, Somerset BA11 1DS
United Kingdom
www.doublecluck.com

Cover design and interior design by Helen Crawford-White
Typeset by Dorchester Typesetting Group Ltd
Printed and bound in Great Britain by CPI Group (UK) Ltd,
Croydon, CR0 4YY
The paper used in this Chicken House book is made from wood
grown in sustainable forests.

1 3 5 7 9 10 8 6 4 2

British Library Cataloguing in Publication data available.

ISBN 978-1-908435-62-0

'. . . there rose suddenly out of the vast gloom of the moor that strange cry which I had already heard upon the borders of the great Grimpen Mire. It came with the wind through the silence of the night, a long, deep mutter, then a rising howl, and then the sad moan in which it died away. Again and again it sounded, the whole air throbbing with it, strident, wild, and menacing.'

Sir Arthur Conan Doyle, *The Hound of the Baskervilles*

gabbleratchet • noun **1** wild geese flying clamorously at night. **2** the Wild Hunt.
— ORIGIN a corruption of *Gabriel* or from Anglo-Saxon *gabbara* or *gabares* 'corpse' + Middle English *racche* or *rache* 'hound'.

1

Matt

Eleven forty-seven. Already the train was slowing into Exeter station and my options were dwindling to a big fat nothing. As the platform approached, I wondered for the millionth time if I'd made a huge mistake in coming here. Uncle Jack hadn't sounded exactly welcoming on the phone. But I'd been so determined to get away from Mum and Paul the four-eyed pillock that I hadn't let it worry me. Now was another matter. I hoped I'd imagined the coldness in his voice when I'd said I needed somewhere to stay. Forget butterflies in my stomach – they'd turned into giant carnivorous moths.

For a second or two I toyed with the idea of

going back to London. Then I steeled myself, heaved my bag on to my shoulder and stepped out of the train.

It was only till the end of half term – a week and a bit. I could manage that, couldn't I? Though to hear Mum panicking you'd think I was heading into unmapped jungle. She couldn't believe it when I'd announced the day before that I'd rung Uncle Jack and was going there whether she liked it or not. But what else could I do? With Dad off sailing, my bolt-hole had disappeared. There was no way I was staying in our house with Paul acting as if he owned it. I had to get as far away as possible, and Uncle Jack's was the only place left to escape to – all my friends are off with their parents doing fun things for the holiday. You know, like normal families do.

I stared up at the clock in the station. Was anyone coming?

Twelve and a half minutes after the train had left, Uncle Jack finally rocked up, looking hassled.

'Goodness, there you are, Matthew,' he said in a sharp voice, as if it was me who was late, not him. He peered at me from under windswept grey hair that matched his grey beard. He looked pretty much how I remembered him, even though it was ages since I'd seen him last. It dawned on me that I scarcely knew him.

'It *is* Matthew, isn't it?' he said. 'Gone quiet, have you? What are you now, thirteen? That's right, isn't it? A year older than Tilda.'

I mumbled a hello and that seemed to be enough for him. He didn't ask me how I was. As he led me over to his clapped-out Land Rover he glanced at his watch. It was obvious he had better things to do than look after me. And I'd just about forced him to take me in. What had I been thinking of? My armpits prickled with embarrassment.

'Your mum all right, then?' he asked suddenly, as we climbed into the Land Rover.

'Suppose so,' I said, and lapsed into silence. I didn't mean to be rude but Uncle Jack didn't seem to notice. He switched on the radio and got on with the driving. At least he had the decency not to bring up why I was here.

And then, just as I was beginning to calm down, we were on the moor.

Imagine a wilderness that goes on and on and on. Acre after acre of desolate landscape covered in dead bracken. That was Dartmoor. It could easily win first prize as the most boring place in the universe. And I'd *chosen* to come here. *Insisted* on it. Only now, the thought of being stuck here for more than a day – no, more than half an hour – was doing my head in. And it was all Paul's fault. But anything had to be better than home.

I'd been here before, just not for a very long time, not since way before Aunty Rose died. I didn't remember much of it. The farm, obviously, and the cows and the sheep. A muddy walk into the depths of nowhere that ended with Mum and Aunty Rose having an argument.

It was strange that we'd hardly ever visited, especially with Dad keeping a boat on the river at Dartmouth, only thirty miles away. And ever since Aunty Rose died I hadn't set eyes on Uncle Jack, or my cousins, Tilda and Kitty. Though to tell the truth, I know why. Mum didn't get on with her sister, though she doesn't talk about it. And she really, really hates Dartmoor, even though she grew up here. She says it gives her the creeps.

We passed a white building, the first sign of civilisation I'd seen in a while. From behind its walls rose a storm of frenzied barking, and I jumped.

'The Hunt kennels,' said Uncle Jack, glancing at me. 'Foxhounds. They're probably being fed. The farmers round here give them the dead livestock.'

'What, like horses and cows?' I said, revolted.

'Mainly all the calves we can't sell.' He gave a short, impatient laugh. 'What did you think they'd get? Pedigree Chum?'

I shut up, and stared ahead at the long twisting road over the moor, stretching into nowhere.

All of a sudden something huge and dark hurtled past my ear and into the car. I yelled out – I couldn't help it – and Uncle Jack swerved violently. A black bird was inside, slamming frantically against the rear window, struggling to find a way out. The car was filled with flapping wings and terrible raucous shrieks.

'Wind your window down! Wind it down!' Uncle Jack was shouting, and I was trying to, but not fast enough.

The bird flew wildly back to the windscreen and then smack into Uncle Jack's face. Ahead, I could see the boulder coming towards us at speed. We hit it with a crunch and the car engine cut out.

I opened my door and tumbled out on to soggy bracken at the side of the road. In a whoosh of black, the bird was out of the car and gone.

Uncle Jack sat in the front seat for what seemed like ages. Then he got out and inspected the damage.

There was a big dent at the front of the Land Rover, but the car was so old I didn't think it mattered much. He gave a heavy sigh, glared at me and got back in again.

'Infernal pest,' he said, and for a moment I wondered whether he meant me or the bird. 'Are you all right?'

I nodded. It was all I could do.

'Come on, then. Let's get to the farm.'

Back in the Land Rover, I shrank into my seat. My heart was thumping and I could still feel the bird's frantic wings against my face. I was sure Uncle Jack blamed me for veering off the road. Why had I ever wanted to come here? It was a horrible place.

We soon turned off on to a tiny lane, with high hedges that cut off all the light. And there, at the bottom of a hollow, was Parson's Farm – a low grey stone building with a slate roof and tiny little windows, surrounded by rickety old barns. Everything seemed too close together for comfort, crammed into the hollow as if breathing was the last thing people needed to worry about.

My cousin Tilda appeared at the front door of the farmhouse as we drove up. She didn't look like the annoying little kid who'd tagged along after me any more. Now she was tall, perhaps almost as tall as me, and her dark red hair was piled on the top of her head in a kind of untidy fountain. She watched us get out of the car, with one hand at the neck of a huge black dog that looked disturbingly like a wolf, and this massive scowl on her face. Uncle Jack called her over, but she didn't bother to move.

The smell of the farm hit me as I picked my way through the puddles, and I just about gagged. How could they stand this stink of manure? It was gross. Tilda just stood there, curling her lip and staring at my trainers like they were alien beings. And there was nothing wrong with them, let me tell you – they were brand-new and pretty nice. It wasn't as if she had anything to be smug about in her mud-spattered wellingtons and mud-coloured coat. In fact, if you left out the pale face and violent red hair she could have been auditioning as a swamp.

Finally she looked up at me.

'Thought you were coming to some posh party, did you?' she said. Then she turned and disappeared inside, the hairy hound following her like she was a plate of pork chops. I was so taken aback I didn't know whether to walk in after her or turn around and go home.

Uncle Jack rolled his eyes. 'She'll be OK later,' he

said. 'I'm sure you'll get on fine.' He didn't sound as if he believed it. 'Well, you're here now. Let's get you installed.'

He clomped into the farmhouse, leaving me to carry my bag on my own. Reluctantly, I trailed into a dark hallway. A wooden sideboard was heaped with clutter, and there were boots and coats everywhere. I followed Uncle Jack up a narrow staircase covered with tatty fraying carpet.

The room I'd be staying in faced out back on to a little vegetable garden, then fields. In the far distance to the left I could make out a purplish patch of wood, and closer in, a grim old stack of stones on top of a hill. I know about this – it's a tor, a load of eroded granite left by the ice. Geography last year, Mr Perrin, 72 per cent. After design and technology, definitely my best subject.

'Are all these fields yours, then?' I said, politely.

Uncle Jack wheeled round and stared at me. He took so long to answer I wondered if he'd heard me right.

'Some of them,' he said. 'Not many. The farm's . . . shrunk a bit recently.' He put his hands in his pockets. 'Right, I'll leave you to settle in. I've got to see to the cows.'

In other words, *Get on with it, you're on your own now.* So much for blood being thicker than water. If only I could change my mind – but it was too late now. I was stuck here.

The room was pretty old-fashioned: faded cream-and-brown flowery wallpaper and an iron bedstead with a cover in every colour under the sun, the kind your granny might have knitted if she had a lorryload of wool and plenty of time on her hands. There was a huge dark wardrobe with carvings on it, a chest of drawers, a couple of shelves full of old nature books, and a stool beside the bed with a frilly lampshade that was frankly embarrassing. That was it. No telly. No computer. Even worse, my phone had no bars at all.

There wasn't much to do but unpack. I shoved my clothes away and tucked my ship's flag into a loose piece of cable at the top of the wall. And finally my camera and my phone. That was the lot.

I went to the window and stared out. As I was wishing I was back in London, or anywhere else in the whole of Britain except here, the door burst open. Almost buried in a giant-sized navy fleece was a small girl in rainbow-patched jeans with a tousled halo of red-gold hair. My cousin Kitty. She'd been a baby when I'd last come here, but now she looked about five.

'You're Matt,' she accused me, plumping herself on to the bed. 'Do you like this?' She patted the lurid cover that *had* to be some sort of hideous family heirloom. 'My granny made it before I was born.' Got that one right, at least.

'Well, it's a bit more . . . homey than I'm used to,' I said guardedly.

Kitty beamed like a demented frog. 'I put it there,' she said. 'I wanted it to be all nice for you.'

At least *someone* in the Parson family was looking out for me.

'What's that?' She was prowling round the room, checking out my additions. The ship's flag had caught her eye.

'It's a burgee, for a sailing boat,' I said. 'A flag. It was my dad's, from the racing club he belonged to.'

'Why have you got it?' Kitty asked.

I shrugged. 'It's old. He was going to throw it away so I kept it.'

'Why?'

To my horror I could feel tears sneaking their way into the corners of my eyes. I blinked them back fast.

'Look, I just did.' It came out a bit sharp, but I

wasn't exactly going to tell her that Dad had left the burgee behind when he cleared out of our house eighteen months ago. I'd salvaged it from the box of his things Mum was chucking in the bin.

Kitty switched tack abruptly. 'Let's go downstairs and have some juice,' she said. 'Come on.'

It wasn't like I had a better offer right now.

'Yeah, OK then,' I said.

Kitty took me down to their vast bare kitchen. Compared to ours, it looked like it came from another century – no units, no steel, just ancient pine cupboards and painted wooden shelves laden with heaps of crockery. It all looked a bit dusty.

Kitty clambered on to a stool and handed me a couple of mismatched glasses. 'Take these,' she instructed. 'And one for Tilda. I'll call her.'

Probably not a good idea, I thought, but I kept it to myself.

Tilda slouched down in response to Kitty's bellow. The faithful hairy hound followed her. Joined at the hip, those two. That must be what happens when you have 368 square miles of wilderness instead of a social life.

'There's biscuits,' said Kitty, 'but only custard creams.'

I helped myself to one.

'How long are you staying?' asked Tilda, her arms folded across her chest.

'All of half term, I think, unless my dad gets home sooner.'

'Great,' she said flatly. She couldn't have summoned up more enthusiasm if I'd been a cockroach.

I didn't get it – why was she being like this? It wasn't like I'd done anything to her, apart from refusing to play with her when we were kids – and, now I come to think of it, putting worms down her back one summer. But that was a long time ago.

'Why aren't you staying with your mum?' said Tilda, her eyes narrow and hard. 'Why do you have to land on us?'

I felt my stomach clench.

'It's because your mum's gone off with someone else, isn't it?' she went on. 'Like, your new dad.'

I couldn't believe she'd just come out with that. My forehead started to burn.

'Shut up,' I said. 'Just shut up.'

I could feel my hand shaking and I put down my glass with a clank, upsetting the carton of juice. It pooled on the wooden table and began dripping over the edge.

Kitty sat open-mouthed. Tilda was smiling. A dark patch of liquid expanded slowly on the red stone floor.

I pushed my chair back so hard it fell over, then I walked out and slammed the door.

2

Tilda

'I wouldn't be doing this if Dad hadn't made me, but he did, so I am,' I said to the door of Matt's bedroom.

Matt hadn't even emerged for lunch. We got out the chocolate flapjacks but he didn't show, so I ate the last of them. Tough, I thought, but Dad told me we had to be kind to poor little city boy or else. I said that if he didn't want to live in his fancy house then maybe he should stay with one of his posh townie friends instead of us. Dad sighed and told me to get upstairs and apologise for having upset him, pronto. So here I was.

City boy made me pay, mind you. First he wouldn't open the door. Then when I kept on knocking for about five minutes, really hard, he opened it so fast that I just about fell into the room.

'Go on, then, say sorry if that's what Daddy wants,' he snapped at me as I tried to get my balance back.

His dark hair was all ruffled and he looked a bit red-eyed, which was kind of pathetic for a thirteen-year-old, I thought.

'Well, you know. Sorry.' Fingers crossed, of course.

'Is that it?'

'Sorry I said that about you coming here. Anyway, it's all your mum's fault.'

He glared at me. 'No it isn't,' he said. 'It was me who refused to stay with Mum when Dad's away. Not while Paul the pillock's there. So you've only got me to blame.'

True enough.

'Where is your dad now?' I asked.

'I don't know exactly – he's not calling much when he's at sea. He was supposed to be in the Canaries this week, but they made a detour to the Azores so it's all taking longer than he planned.'

'Azores?' I said. 'What are they when they're at home? Some kind of disease?'

He shot me a sarky look. 'A bunch of islands in the Atlantic Ocean, dummy.'

'Oh,' I said. I remembered Dad telling me Matt's quite a good sailor himself – he's done a lot of racing with his dad. Not that I could care less. 'And then he's got to sail all the way back to England?'

'No, he's flying back from the Canaries. He wanted to go for longer, only Mum wouldn't let him. But it might take him a week to get there now, maybe two.'

I smiled sweetly. 'But whether he's home or not, you're going to have to go back to Mummy and the pillock boyfriend when school starts, aren't you? I mean, you can't stay here for ever.'

Direct hit. City boy looked completely stricken. Serves him right, I thought. He should never have come in the first place – he must know that, surely. I mean, his family and ours have hardly spoken for ages. Though Mum did talk to Aunty Caroline the day before her accident – I remember her coming off the phone really angry. And Aunty Caroline didn't even bother going to the funeral – her own sister. Then there's the question of the farm and what will happen to it now, and thinking about that makes me so furious I can't speak.

But we haven't got much choice about Matt staying, for a few days at least – unless we put him out on to the moor and leave him for the wolves to find. Too bad there aren't any now, just ponies and cows and sheep.

'Dad says I have to show you round,' I said. 'It's a farm, so you can't be a complete disaster area. But you'll have to put on boots instead of those stupid things.'

When we finally got outside – Matt in this fashion-victim jacket, but wearing Dad's wellies – I took him on the grand tour of our three yards. The front yard first, with East and West Barn – they're empty just now, but we use West Barn for lambing in the spring, and the cows'll be coming into East Barn for the winter soon. Matt yawned, but I ignored him.

Then I led him into the back yard where the chickies have their house. I called them over for a bit of corn, and my favourites, Flo and Mabel, started pecking from my hand.

'Want to give them some?' I asked, thinking he might as well learn to help out with the chores. I offered him the jug, but he pushed it away.

'No chance,' he said. 'They've got evil eyes. Like velociraptors.'

'You're not scared of a little chicken, are you?'

'I'm serious. Chickens are the closest living relatives of Tyrannosaurus rex.'

He had a point. When chickens run, they *are* kind of Jurassic Park.

'Let's go and see the rest then.' I whistled for Jez, who came bounding up.

'The hairy hound,' Matt said. 'What is it?'

'It's a she, and she's a black German shepherd,' I said. 'Jezebel, Jez for short. She's really clever.'

Jez smiled her doggy smile and danced ahead. Matt didn't make any move to pet her. I was starting to realise he might not be the animal type. Not a good omen, if you ask me.

'We've got two puppies as well, but they're only on loan,' I said. 'They're outside dogs, not house dogs. Round here.' I led him across the back yard to the tractor barn. 'Watch out. They're really naughty.'

It was too late. Lightfoot and Lawless had leapt up from their straw bed and were jumping all over Matt. They were almost full grown now – tall and strong and far too badly behaved. Matt kept trying to fend their huge paws off his jacket, but I knew it was a lost cause. It was hilarious.

'Don't worry, they won't kill you,' I said. 'They're foxhounds – we're looking after them for the Hunt. Down, Lightfoot. Oh, get off, Lawless.'

I pushed off the puppies and stroked their

squirming tummies.

'You mean those kennels down the road have dogs for fox hunting?' said Matt.

'Duh. Yes. Loads of farmers take a couple of puppies and train them to be sociable, then they go back and join the pack and start hunting. Following a scent that the Hunt's laid down, that is, not chasing actual foxes any more, so don't look so shocked. But we don't like foxes in the country. Especially when we have lambs and chickens and geese. I suppose you're all anti up in London.'

'Yeah, well, we're not all out for blood like you obviously are here.'

I laughed, shut the puppies up and started on the tour again. I showed him the rest of the back yard but he barely glanced at all the machinery in the tractor barn. I did my best, piling it on thick about animal emergencies and having to stick your hand up a ewe's bum. Only he didn't seem much interested in anything. I decided to give the side yard and the geese a miss for now.

'OK,' I said. 'Let's go up to Coven Tor – you'll have seen it from your window. We'll pass by Far Field on the way, and say hello to the sheep there.'

Matt shrugged and we headed over to the front of

the house again. Gabe, who helps Dad on the farm, was up at the main gate, shifting hurdles. I tried to sneak past him without catching his eye but he wasn't having any of it.

'Off somewhere?' he said.

'Just to the tor,' I said. 'We're in a bit of a hurry.'

Gabe frowned at Matt.

'Caroline's boy, isn't it?' he said. 'I saw you when you were small once. She doesn't come here now she lives upcountry.'

He eyed Matt like he was figuring out how much he'd fetch at market. Matt shifted uneasily.

'I'm Matt Crimmond,' he said. 'Pleased to meet you.' He stuck out a hand, but Gabe didn't seem to notice it. I don't think he's used to city-boy manners.

'Gabe Tucker,' he said. 'I work on the farm here. You be careful of the moor now, boy. It's a dangerous place, and I don't just mean the weather. There's dark things happen here.' He muttered a word under his breath that I'd never heard before. Gabble-something or other. Gobbledegook, more like.

Matt was looking a bit puzzled, which was fair enough really. Gabe's kind of odd at the best of times, though his wife Alba's dead nice and used to be my favourite dinner lady.

'Got to go,' I said. I waved and pushed Matt through the gate.

'What did he mean?' Matt asked in a low voice as we walked away down the farm track past Long Field. 'And what's the gabble thingy when it's at home?'

'I've no idea, and anyway, it's not worth the effort. He's always like that,' I said.

'Like what?'

'Oh, you know. Death and destruction.' I put on a gruff Gabe-like voice. '"Strange things happen on the moor, stranger than you can imagine." He's obsessed with these weird stories everyone used to believe in round here. That's why he gave me Jez when she was a puppy – to protect me from bad things. Bonkers.'

Matt was frowning. 'Don't you get a bit spooked out, though?' he said. 'I mean, being all on your own with nothing for miles around? It's sort of creepy. And lots of those barns on the farm look like they've come straight out of a horror movie. You know, rotting planks, creaking doors . . .'

I flinched. 'Yeah, and why do you think they're in such a bad state? The same reason we've lost all our best fields.'

'Your dad mentioned that,' Matt said. 'Hey, maybe it's time to get out of farming.'

The arrogant pig! I couldn't believe it. Surely he knows that it's because of his mum we're going to lose the farm? It's her fault we had to sell off all that land, just before Mum died. That's why the farm's struggling now – we've lost all the best pasture. Dad had said I had to be nice, but suddenly I just couldn't do it any more.

'The farm's my home,' I said, and my voice came out like a hiss. 'So why don't you just get lost and leave us all alone?'

'What's up with you?' Matt said, but I pulled my hood up and marched back along the track towards the house.

Beyond the gate, Gabe watched us, slowly shaking his head.

3

Matt

In the end I trailed back to the farm as well. What was Tilda's problem? I was totally confused, but sort of hurt, too. To make things worse, that Gabe bloke grabbed me as I was coming into the front yard and said he wanted a word with me. I couldn't refuse but I wasn't exactly keen – he weirds me out a bit. He must be nearly sixty, I think, and he wears this dirty-looking beanie hat down to his eyebrows, and under it his eyes are really hard and pale, a pale blue you don't normally see. And right now he was acting all secretive, like he was trying to drag me into some bizarre conspiracy.

'Listen to me, now,' he said. 'I saw you back there,

you and Tilda, having words. This is the beginning. I know it. If you carry on like this, you'll set it off again.'

'The beginning of what?' I said, trying to shake my arm free.

Gabe's eyes shifted away.

'What is it?' I said. 'What will we set off?'

'It'll be birds first, I reckon. They're the omens. The harbingers.'

'Harbingers?' What was he on about? I looked around, wondering how to get rid of him, but he kept going.

'They'll be gathering now,' he said. 'Watching, waiting. I felt it when your uncle told me you were coming. And now I know it. If you've any sense you'll get away from here as fast as you can. Before you bring on something worse than birds.'

He saw me smile and a flicker of what might have been anger passed across his eyes.

'Just stay away from Old Scratch Wood,' he said, 'and maybe you'll be OK. If you're lucky – and there's plenty enough ill luck here.'

Wacko. Some people have spent far too long away from normal life – and that includes pretty much the whole population of Dartmoor, I should think. When the most exciting thing you have to look forward to is a trip to the sheep market, you obviously start going a bit psycho.

'I'm sure you're right,' I said. 'I'll look out for these omens. Harbingers. Whatever.'

He threw me a glance of pure contempt.

'Best you do that, Matt Crimmond,' he said. 'Because I'm afraid they'll be looking out for you.'

The sun went in and for some reason my guts churned uncomfortably. But it seemed that Gabe had said all he was going to say. He turned and went off into one of the barns in front of the farm – East Barn, I think Tilda had called it. There were so many of them I couldn't remember.

I dragged my feet up to the gloomy old house. Gabe was nuts, obviously. But after the bust-up with Tilda, I sort of wished he'd kept his nuttiness to himself.

Just as I reached the door, a car drew up to the gate. Tilda rushed rudely past me out to the lane and got into the back with another girl. Uncle Jack came out to wave goodbye, then told me she was going over to Widecombe and wouldn't be back till late. Why was she avoiding me like this? When she was showing me around, she was almost pleasant one minute, the next she was acting like a mental case. It wasn't like I said anything out of order – she just went off on one. I didn't get it.

Once I was in, things improved. Uncle Jack said the farm computer was off limits except for emergencies, but I could watch TV for a while. Finally Kitty trotted up and announced that we'd better all have a wash and then it would be time for supper. When I say it like that it sounds a bit Famous Five, but she was just being nice. And believe me, I needed some of that.

Amazingly, she'd even laid the table in the kitchen – this huge old pine number, all scuffed and ringed from stuff that had been spilt on it and scrubbed away. It should have looked rubbish, but it didn't. Just sort of homely. Kitty had set out mats and forks and knives and salt and pepper and everything. My mum would be seriously impressed – she says I never do anything around the house. Then Uncle Jack came in and brought something out of the range cooker, and when he took the lid off, it wasn't a burnt offering like I would have expected from him, but this casserole with dark purplish gravy and a fantastic meaty smell that had me almost dribbling on to the flagstones. I hadn't eaten since breakfast, thanks to Tilda, and now I realised just how hungry I was.

'This is Hector,' said Uncle Jack, waving his fork at

the casserole. *He's totally lost it, too,* I thought.

Kitty grinned at me. 'Hector was one of our bullocks,' she said. 'I didn't like him a lot because he had a bad temper. But he tastes nice.'

We're on first name terms with our dinner? Still . . . I only hesitated a nanosecond, then dived in. And Hector was amazing. I'd never really thought about where the meat we eat at home comes from – but this tasted way better. We ate him with big hunks of bread, which we tore off and dipped in the gravy to mop it up. My mum would have had a fit at our lack of manners, but it really was great stuff.

There wasn't a lot being said apart from 'Pass the butter,' but once I'd staved off the first pangs of hunger I thought I'd try to find out what Gabe had been ranting on about.

'The bloke that works on the farm mentioned Old Scratch Wood,' I said. 'He told me not to go there.'

Uncle Jack looked up from a forkful of Hector and pushed his hair back from his eyes. Suddenly I could see a resemblance to Tilda.

'Gabe?' he said. 'What else did he say about it?'

'I don't know, really. He was going on about omens or harbingers or something.'

'Oh, you don't want to pay too much attention to

27

Gabe's stories,' said Uncle Jack curtly, and went back to his supper.

I squirmed in my seat.

'What's barbingers?' said Kitty.

Uncle Jack actually smiled.

'They foretell that something is coming, darling,' he said. 'Like I can foretell that it's nearly your bedtime.' Kitty obviously had a good effect on him, because as he turned to me I could see he was already in a better mood. 'Gabe likes to ladle on the local colour – he's a walking folklore museum,' he said. 'But Old Scratch Wood is just a small wood on the moor beyond Thieves' Tor. Not much left of it now, although it's very old. One of the last native forests in England. The oaks there are ancient. Quite strange-looking . . .'

'Can we have pudding now?' said Kitty.

'Yes, sweetheart,' said Uncle Jack. 'I'll get out the treacle tart in a minute. But maybe you should go there, Matthew. It'll be something for you to do, now you're here.' He gave me a probing look. 'I'll get Tilda to take you tomorrow.'

I tried a dutiful guest smile, but a day out with Tilda wasn't quite what I was after.

'Can I go, too?' said Kitty.

It was all I could do not to pull a face. Kitty was all

right, but I didn't fancy dragging a five-year-old across the moor as well as a moody Tilda. Thankfully Uncle Jack came to my rescue.

'Your legs are a bit small for that,' he said. Kitty's face fell. 'But you can come and help me muck out the chickens.' Apparently this was a major treat for Kitty, because her lip stopped quivering immediately.

So. Just me and Tilda in the middle of the big bad wood. I couldn't wait.

'Right,' said Uncle Jack, standing up. 'Enough of this. Make yourself useful now, Matthew, and get on with the washing-up while I put Kitty to bed.'

I looked to see if he was joking, but he wasn't. There was no dishwasher, just a great pile of dirty dishes and disgusting pans. Uncle Jack raised a warning eyebrow and I thought better of making an excuse. Slowly I moved towards the sink and turned on the hot water.

It all took ages, even though Uncle Jack came and helped with the drying and the putting-away. It was clear he was thinking about something, and occasionally I could feel his eyes on me. When the last dish had disappeared, I made myself break the silence.

'I meant to say before – I'm sorry about Aunty Rose. She was really nice.'

Uncle Jack's face darkened. He picked up the tea

towel, folded it over the rail of the range and headed for the door.

'I've got to be up at crack of dawn, so I'm only fit for the TV now,' he said in a tired voice. 'Oh, and ring your mother, won't you? She called for you earlier. Said she couldn't get through on your phone.'

I hesitated, then followed him to the living room. I hovered at the door, unsure what to do. Uncle Jack had crashed out on the sofa in front of the box to watch some boring sitcom. There was another old armchair beside the wood burner, but after the look he'd given me I felt nervous about coming in, and he didn't ask me to. In moments he was snoring away – and it was only eight o'clock.

No one wanted me here, that much was obvious. I felt desperate to talk to someone. Maybe I could get reception for my phone out in the front yard. But I wasn't going to ring my mum – no way.

I stuck on Uncle Jack's wellies again, and an old fleece that was hanging by the door. Then I crept out.

Straight away I was glad that I had. The moon was amazing – huge and low on the horizon, and about three-quarters full. You could almost see all its scars and craters and bumps and hollows. You don't get that in London. I stood admiring it, feeling a bit stupid as

I waved my phone around to find a spot that would let me at least pick up my messages. From the back yard came a low moo and a loud burst of clucking, shattering the silence. No signal, though. I'd have to go further away.

Higher ground would be best, I reckoned. I would try the tor I'd seen from my room. I went out of the front gate, remembering to close it behind me, and followed the farm track past Long Field where Tilda had taken me that afternoon. At the end of the field was a ridge with a well-worn path on it that looked as if it led through the fields at the back of the farm, and right to the top. With the moon so bright, I could easily make out the silhouettes of the stone stacks – three of them, like heaped piles of giant sheep poo left on top of a hill. I took a quick picture with my phone, not that it was likely to come out in this light, but if I was going to be marooned here I might as well have something to show for it.

Despite the fleece I was really cold. I concentrated on getting to the top as fast as possible, only it wasn't as easy it looked. By the time I reached the stones I was panting. And still no reception. I groaned. If I couldn't even get texts while I was here, it was going to be truly dire.

It was then I heard it. In the distance, a low rhythmic sound, almost like a train, though even I know you don't get trains in the middle of Dartmoor. Especially not in the sky.

I looked up, and saw several dark shapes flying past, way up high in the air. Geese, big ones, black against the moon. The beat of their wings grew louder, and they were honking away, or whatever it is geese do. It was sort of eerie. I watched them disappear into the night, feeling cold to my bone marrow. The sound held on the wind, growing higher and higher, then faded away.

Everything was silent now – horribly, creepily silent in a way you never get in a city. I found myself missing the non-stop noise of London, wishing desperately that I was back there, even though it didn't really feel like home any more now that Paul had moved in. Then a cloud passed over the moon, and suddenly I was in darkness. The rocks in front of me seemed to grow about ten feet. The path disappeared. I could hear myself breathing way too fast. What an idiot I was for not having brought a torch, I thought. With shaking fingers I held up my phone and its feeble light.

It must have been a minute or two before the moon

cleared and my heart rate slowed. I didn't waste any time in heading back down the path, though I managed not to run. But I admit I wanted to, pretty badly.

Uncle Jack was still on the sofa, dead to the world, and Tilda hadn't come back yet. I tried to have a bath in the freezing bathroom upstairs, but the water ran cold before it reached about ten centimetres. In the end I gave up and sloped off to bed. To be honest, I was totally done in.

Even though I'd turned my nose up at it earlier, I was quite glad of the crochet cover because it was freezing in my room too. There was an ancient radiator but it didn't seem to be pumping out any heat. In the end I put my socks back on, and a jumper over my pyjamas. I lay there shivering for a while, listening to the sounds outside. First an owl – I'd never heard a real one before but you can't mistake it. Then something flying over, making a huge racket – a sort of low honking bark. More geese, I supposed, like the ones I'd just seen up on the tor. That, or a huge pack of flying dogs. Everything was blurring together now. And in seconds I was asleep.

4

Tilda

A Sunday's no different on a farm – you still have to get up and feed the animals, but that obviously hadn't occurred to Matt. His door was firmly shut. *Making sure of his beauty sleep*, I thought crossly. I gave Jez her food and a bit of a cuddle. Then I put out mash for the chickies and wheat for the geese, and changed their water and saw to the puppies. Finally I came back inside to get the breakfast ready.

It's times like this when I really miss Mum. She used to cook us bacon and eggs on Sundays, sometimes with pancakes and maple syrup. There was always a fire in the grate and Radio 4 in the background, and she'd make a point of taking us out on nature walks even though Dad usually had to do stuff on the farm. Since she died, a lot of that's been up to me, and I'm not much good at any of it. Dad says I am, but I know he's just trying to make me feel all right.

Anyway, I thought I'd impress him and scramble some eggs. Some of the hens are still laying well, even though it's nearly November now. I sell quite a few at the farm gate when we have a glut, to make a bit of extra pocket money, along with sweet peas in the summer – Mum's favourite. I wished she could have seen them this year. But then, I wished a lot of stuff, all the time. I wished she'd stayed home that day of the accident. Nothing was fair. The worst thing of all was that I was finding it harder and harder to remember her face any more. But it was no use feeling sorry for myself – I had to be strong for Dad and Kitty.

This morning Kitty was eager-beavering away in the kitchen and she helped me get everything ready. Then Dad came in, starving as usual because he'd been out in the fields. I got the eggs to a perfect consistency, not too hard, not too soft, and doled them out. City boy hadn't bothered to make an appearance yet, but I put his on a plate, too. If he couldn't get up on time he could just eat it cold.

I was glad I'd found an excuse to disappear last night with my friend Amy, and today I decided that the less I saw of Matt the better. Then Dad hit me with it: Matt was asking about Old Scratch Wood, so I was to take him out and show him around – no wriggling out of it. I said I was busy, but Dad wasn't having any arguments. He did his super-stern face and said it was either that or no pocket money, so I knew there was no point moaning.

It wasn't till we were finishing up our coffee that city boy showed. No apology or anything – he just walked in, yawning, sat down at the table and said hi. Like he expected someone to jump up and run around after him. Well, it wasn't going to be me.

'Your breakfast is over there,' Dad said, pointing at the range.

Matt looked a bit surprised but went and collected his eggs – nicely congealed, I noted. Dad said he was sorry but he had to go out again, and was Kitty going to help him?

'Are you mucking out the chickies?' she said.

'Only the best jobs for you, darling,' said Dad, and she jumped up and shot out of the door after him.

So now it was just Matt and me. Great.

'Apparently I've got to take you to Old Scratch

36

Wood,' I said.

Matt sounded bored. 'Don't strain yourself,' he said. 'I'm not that interested.'

'Well, Dad told me you were really keen. He says I've got to show you around now you're here. It'll have to be later, though. I've got stuff to do. Farms take a lot of work. Speaking of which, there's plenty of washing-up.' And I left him to the dishes.

Round about midday, I shoved together a couple of pasties, some apples and a bar of chocolate. Then I had an idea. I ran upstairs, pulled something out from the back of the wardrobe and stuffed it into my rucksack. I smiled to myself.

Jez knew she was going on a walk – she's super-intelligent like that – and started barking away, so I went to get Matt. He was sitting in his bedroom staring out the window. Pathetic. But he came down when I called him, and he even asked if he could borrow Dad's spare boots. I'd been kind of hoping he'd forget – the moor would have completely ruined his precious trainers.

We left the puppies for Dad to walk – they're just too much of a handful right now. They've got so big, and they're not properly trained like Jez is, because they'll be acting as a pack when they go off to the

Hunt. Dad quite likes having them, all the same – he says it's only neighbourly, what with the kennels being so near.

Gabe was hanging around again as we went out. I tried to give him the swerve but he headed straight towards us with his pitchfork in his hand, like the grim reaper or something. He had his music on and I could hear the tinny sound of Black Sabbath, the rubbish old heavy metal band that seems to be the only thing he ever plays.

'Hi Gabe,' I said cheerily. 'How's Alba getting on with the salsa dancing?'

This was a bit cheeky of me, I knew. Gabe's wife Alba has started going out twice a week to the village hall in a short skirt and it's been driving Gabe mad. He didn't take the bait, though.

'I know where you're off to, Tilda Parson,' he said, taking out his earbuds. 'And I know perfectly well you don't pay any attention to what I say. You haven't got the sense you were born with.'

'Don't panic,' I said, stifling a giggle. 'We're just going to look round the edge, and then we're coming straight back.'

He stared at me, then put the earbuds back in and shambled off towards the back yard.

Matt wasn't looking happy as we trudged through the front gate and out on to the moor. I bet he really hates walking. He probably spends all his time on the smelly old Underground.

It's quite a long way to Old Scratch Wood. We went past Long Field on the farm track, then the field that isn't ours any more, with Far Field behind it. I asked Matt if he wanted to see the sheep, but he wasn't interested, so we crossed over the road that goes to Widecombe and on to the bridle path that cuts round Thieves' Tor. I'm used to going everywhere on foot with Jez, but Matt kept moaning about it, asking me how long till we got there, like a kid in the back of a car. He's so annoying.

The moor's fine so long as you know where you're going and stick to the footpaths, but only if it's good weather. Loads of people have got lost when the fog's come down, and frozen to death, or strayed into mires and been sucked down under the mud. Dad says, 'Pay the moor respect, and she'll let you alone,' and insists I always carry a compass. I told Matt this, and he laughed his head off.

'Yeah, well, if you're so clever, take a landmark now and we'll see how well it holds up,' I said.

Matt shrugged and locked on to the road behind us

and the tor in front to get his bearings. Then I led him over a few hillocks and off the bridle path. We tramped through the soggy tangle of bracken and stunted gorse bushes. They were blooming yellow even though it was late in the year.

'Kissing still going strong, then,' I said, and then felt my cheeks turn hot as Matt stared at me.

'*When the gorse is not in bloom, then kissing's not in fashion*,' I mumbled. 'It's an old country saying. Don't you know anything?'

'Sorry, I must have been away when they did turnip-farming at school,' said Matt.

'OK, then, tell me where we've just come from?'

Matt turned round. The road had disappeared from view behind the hillocks. It looked as if we were miles from anywhere. He glanced at the tor, then did a double take. There were now two tors in the distance. The stacks of grey stone rose up on either side of us, and the bridle path was nowhere to be seen.

'Wow,' said Matt. 'That's pretty strange. I could have sworn that was the tor we were aiming at.' He pointed to the right-hand one. 'But I don't know. Wait. There must be traffic, surely.'

We both listened. No cars. The wind whistled round our ears. Small birds twittered from hiding places among the heather stalks. Jez sniffed around, but didn't find anything.

'That way,' Matt hazarded. I laughed.

'Wrong,' I said. 'That's our tor over there – the higher, fatter one. That's Thieves' Tor. The other one is Hunting Horn Tor. The road's back over there.'

Even I couldn't find the path we had left, so I led him all the way up to the grey stone stacks. The road reappeared down below, exactly where I had said it was.

'Point taken,' Matt mumbled.

'Wait until the fog comes down,' I said. 'Then it doesn't matter how many landmarks you have, you've no chance of finding your way. Unless you've got Jez with you, of course. She knows everywhere round here.'

'So you fall into a bog and if you don't die of hypothermia, you wake up to find you're looking straight into the red eyes of the Hound of the Baskervilles,' said Matt. 'I know. I've seen Sherlock Holmes on the telly.'

'Exactly. So pay attention.'

Matt glanced at me, suddenly serious.

'Do you think it's OK to go to Old Scratch Wood, then?' he asked.

41

'Of course it is.' I looked at him. 'Why? Gabe's got you rattled, has he?' I started to laugh. The idea was hilarious.

'Yeah, all right,' he said. 'Maybe it *is* sort of stupid. But this place creeps me out. There's something strange about it . . .'

What a total killjoy. 'Oh, get over yourself,' I said. 'Stop being such a wuss. Anyway, it's another half an hour to Old Scratch Wood, so save your breath, you'll be needing it.'

We walked on for a while, Jez nosing around ahead of us. Matt looked really hacked off, but he didn't have a choice – he was far too much of a townie to find his own way home. I was having a good time, though. For late October, it was great weather, cold and bright and clear. I love the moor even when it's raining – you can still see birds and animals if you know where to look – but days like this are brilliant. All over the place clumps of dead bracken were glowing orange in the faint sun.

Far away across the moor, a horn sounded two long blasts.

'Wow, the Hunt must be out,' I said. 'What a perfect day for it.'

Matt stared at me as if I was mad. I turned my back

on him and scanned the horizon for riders. Nothing – they must be too far off. Shame. But maybe a good thing too – Matt would only have been snotty about it. I whistled to Jez and tramped on.

When Old Scratch Wood finally appeared, it was a grey-purple mist on the side of a valley with a rushing stream at the bottom. You can just see it in the distance from the back of our house, but up close it's really strange. As we drew nearer, the mist formed into a tight mass of leafless trees, silver against the grey sky. For some reason, we both slowed our steps and began walking on the narrow footpath at the side of the valley. Even Jez quietened down, suddenly glued to my heel.

Only when we were right at the edge of the wood could we make out the oaks' true shapes – stunted, twisted forms, like cartoons of trees drawn by someone with an evil imagination. I'd forgotten how much I disliked the place. Mum's car accident happened somewhere near here, though I don't know exactly where. But it wasn't just that, it was the wood itself. The outer trees were blue-grey with lichen covering every bit of them. Deeper inside the wood, they all had bright green ferns sprouting from their limbs. Every inch of the ground was writing with mossy growths on boulders and broken branches.

'So this is what ancient forest looks like,' said Matt. His voice sounded unnecessarily loud in the silence.

I shivered, though I don't think Matt noticed. 'This is supposed to be the devil's favourite place on Dartmoor,' I said. 'That's what Old Scratch means. It's another name for the devil.'

'Well, if the devil seriously wanted to hang about on earth, I reckon Dartmoor would have to be his first choice,' said Matt.

There he went again. Insulting where I lived, like it was nothing. I plonked myself on a rock.

'Sit, Jez,' I said. She stared at me with disappointment in her brown eyes, but sat down obediently. Then I turned to Matt.

'This is as far as I'm going. You go in by yourself. If you dare.'

'You're not serious, are you?'

'Yes, I am.' I took a bird book out of my rucksack and began to leaf through its pages. Jez settled down beside me, her black nose on my knee.

Matt stared at me, confused.

'OK,' he said at last. 'I'll meet you out here when I've had a look.'

'Watch out for the adders, then.'

'Yeah, right.'

I didn't look up, and he stared some more, then turned and started clambering over the boulders into the forest, his hands scratching for holds on the dank moss. Above him the stunted trees dripped fronds of lichen. I sat still until he disappeared from view. Then I helped myself to a pasty, put the bird book into my pocket and scooted round the perimeter of the wood with Jez to a tiny path I vaguely remembered, which led into the centre. I delved into my rucksack, fished out the special item I'd brought with me and put it in my pocket.

OK, city boy, I thought. *It's show time.*

5

Matt

I'd never seen so much moss in my life. The boulders were covered in it, and everywhere there were huge broken branches wrapped in disgusting green fur. I had to grab the stones because they were so slippery underfoot, so I kept getting a handful of the stuff – wet and cold and repulsive. Up above my head were blue-green clumps and fronds of lichen that looked like they'd been there since time began. Ferns hung from limbs like long hairy curtains. And the trees weren't just short, they were practically horizontal, the branches splayed out low and creepy like twisted arms and hands. It was insane. I'd never seen anything like it.

My imagination was going berserk. I could almost feel the trees eyeing me, as if they were about to bend down and fold me into their trunks. I shook myself. It was all getting a bit *Lord of the Rings*. I knew I was being dumb – they were only trees. Weird ones, yes, but just trees. At home, the only green spaces I ever saw were the London parks. I'd been in forests before, of course – I'd done the whole mushroom-gathering, squirrel-watching, *oh-look-at-all-the-lovely-rotting-timber* thing when I was a kid with my mum and dad, and wasn't exactly thrilled by it then – but never on my own. That was why Old Scratch Wood was giving me the creeps, I told myself. I just wasn't used to it.

I gritted my teeth. I wasn't going to pop out after two minutes only to have Tilda sneering at me. Instead I scrambled deeper into the wood, looking for a path or a clearing. After all, it couldn't be that big – we'd seen it from the top of the valley and it wasn't exactly Sherwood Forest. Uncle Jack had said that most of it had been cut down over the years, and it was true there wasn't much left. It looked like you could probably walk round the whole thing in less than half an hour.

The trouble was that inside it all seemed very different. Darker. Denser. And a whole lot scarier.

I didn't quite know how this had happened. If anyone had said to me, *Hey Matt, fancy a walk on your own through this ancient wood that's apparently one of the devil's favourite places?* I'd have told them to get lost, and fast. But spend an afternoon with my pain of a cousin and suddenly I'm knee-deep in prehistoric jungle while she's sunning herself outside with Jez. To my surprise I found I was missing the hairy hound.

The worst thing was, it was my fault. Gabe had told me not to go to Old Scratch Wood. So like an idiot, what do I end up doing? I had to give it to the old nutter, he was dead right about this one. I couldn't think of anywhere I'd less like to be.

But I wondered why he'd gone on about this place. He'd said something about omens. Birds, was it? Back then it had sounded crazy, but now I wasn't so sure. All round me there were rustlings and twitterings. And now I'd started noticing, I could see two crows perched on a low branch ahead of me. One of them flapped its wings and let out a rasping call. For a second I could see its black tongue protruding. Were they watching for me? I thought of the black bird that had flown into the car when I first arrived and felt a tingling at the top of my spine.

And then there was the strange word Gabe had

used when I first met him – the gabble thingy. I wished I knew what he meant.

Stop thinking like this, I told myself. *Just chill out.*

But I was getting myself well and truly spooked. In the thick of this repulsive wood it felt like something horrible could happen any moment.

All at once something hooked into my hair. I jumped about a foot, hit my head against a branch and got a load of the disgusting lichen all over my face. I tore at my hair and untangled the furry twigs from it, then made myself stand still until my breathing slowed. Just a branch.

'Keep calm,' I said under my breath. 'This is exactly what Tilda wants – to scare you out of your wits.'

I dug my camera from my inside pocket. At least I could get some pictures so I could prove to my mates what I'd had to put up with here. And it would give me something else to think about, too.

I started snapping odd things – a mossy stone, a lichen-dripping branch, a gnarled tree trunk. It was amazing how it all crowded into the frame, this jungle of green twisting forms. Everything was straight out of some fairy-tale illustration of an enchanted forest – the kind you get stuck in for ever.

It was reassuring to hold the camera, though. It

made me feel more normal. My dad had taught me how to get a half-decent picture – he's a really good photographer, though he's never done it professionally. He could have, but he chose architecture instead. He'd like these shots, I reckoned. I climbed on to a high-ish stone and carried on snapping till I had about twenty, then stuck my camera back in my pocket. Some of them looked really good.

Suddenly I wondered about the adders Tilda had mentioned. Were they for real? Probably – this wood seemed like the perfect breeding ground, not that I knew the first thing about reptiles. Maybe they'd prefer it sunny? Still, I started looking down before placing my hands on any more rocks.

I was beginning to think I would go back after all, when just ahead the weirdo trees seemed to thin out, and the sun shone brighter through the branches. Relieved, I made for the patch of light. It wasn't easy; the branches clung to me and scraped my hair and my cheeks. Even the stones shifted under my weight, as if they wanted to topple me over.

At last the trees parted around a clearing filled with light. At its centre stood a huge stone, tall as a tall man and twice as broad. Unlike every other boulder I'd encountered in this wood so far, it was entirely bare of moss. There was something truly strange about it.

Then I realised what it was. A standing stone – a real one, like you get at Stonehenge. But how did it end up here? It must have been dragged in by the druids or some other bunch of loonies, I guessed, and stuck in the middle of the forest. Weird. I wondered what it was for – sacrifices, maybe? I shuddered.

The noises in the wood had changed, too. I slowly became aware of the sound the stream was making down in the valley. Now it was roaring as loud as the sea. I thought of Dad out on the Atlantic and my ears filled with the crashing of imaginary waves. I stepped forward, almost in a trance, my whole body moving to the rhythm of the breakers. There was something about the grey stone that made me want to touch it. Slowly I made for it, pulled towards it like iron filings to a giant magnet.

From behind the stone came a choked snarl.

I froze. My heart was hammering inside my chest. My tongue felt large and dry and alien. I could hear the blood racing in my veins – and surely whatever it was could hear it, too.

Then I saw it in front of me. Some sort of creature. Grey fur. Fangs. A bloody mouth. I screamed. None of my muscles would move. I stood there, hearing the scream resonate round the clearing.

Suddenly Tilda was there beside me, ripping something off her head and grabbing my arm.

'It's OK, Matt,' she said, 'it's only me. Me and . . .' she giggled, '. . .Wally the Werewolf. My Hallowe'en special. For the most haunted place in Britain.'

She was cracking up with laughter now. Totally shaking with it. Jez loped up behind her, doing a wolf impression of her own.

'Your face,' Tilda said. 'It was the best thing I've seen in years. Don't you know that werewolves don't exist, dummy?'

I took it all in: the furry mask, my pig of a cousin, the awfulness of everything. I stepped towards her.

Tilda jerked backwards, then tripped and fell. She lay there, sprawled on the leaf mould that covered the clearing. I didn't wait to see whether she was all right. I could feel tears at the back of my eyes getting ready to do their stuff and was determined that they wouldn't. I turned and stormed into the forest, no longer caring which way I was going. Anywhere so long as it was away from her.

6

Tilda

I listened to city boy's footsteps disappearing into the heart of the wood, expecting him to turn back any minute. He didn't. When I couldn't hear anything more, I tried to pick myself up, but I'd done something to my ankle and it hurt a bit to put weight on it. Quite a lot actually, but there was no way I was going to cry about it. OK, I might have whimpered once or twice, but not much, considering. Jez nosed me and whined, then pushed me with her head as if to say *Get up, now, or else*. I pulled myself together, got on to all fours and crawled towards the standing stone. Jez followed, her feathery tail right down. She hates it when something's up with me.

I'd have to drag myself out on the path – which of course Matt hadn't cottoned on to yet, the numbskull. And then I'd just have to wait until someone came along to help, I supposed, since it was impossible to get a phone signal anywhere round here. I checked my watch. Three thirty. It would be getting dark by six, and nobody in their right mind would want to be in Old Scratch Wood once the sun went down. I'd better be quick.

I'm not frightened by many things, but the thought of spending the night in a so-called haunted wood with only Jez to keep me company was just a little bit scary. Already it had grown colder, even though I was out of the wind here. I could hear the stream thundering down below and all sorts of rustlings in the trees. Invisible birds had started chattering, but I couldn't see a single one. They seemed very close. I wondered if something had maybe panicked them, then tried not to think about it.

I eased my walking boot off and felt my ankle up and down. It was sore, but I knew I hadn't broken it – they say you can hear the bone split if you do that, and I was sure the only sound had been me falling on my bum. Anyway, I'd be screaming my head off if I'd done anything seriously bad to it. I twirled my toes experimentally and then tried rotating my ankle. I could do it – just – but it really hurt.

Then I heard it. A sharp crack, like a broken twig. Instantly Jez stiffened. A shuffling noise overlaid the sound of the stream. Something was creeping up on me from out of the trees.

You know how normally you don't notice your internal organs? Suddenly they were all there and larger than life – stomach, lungs, heart, the works. I could feel my blood hot and violent in my veins. All the saliva had disappeared from my mouth.

Another crack, only nearer. What was it? An animal? I could hear it breathing now, great breathy breaths and scufflings. I looked around wildly, my hands scrabbling on the ground for something to defend myself with. The left one touched a hard metallic edge at the base of the standing stone. Frantic, my fingers dug into the crumbly earth to try and free it. It wouldn't budge. I shut my eyes in panic. Jez barked and barked . . .

Something was leaning over me. I felt its shadow pass over my eyelids and I scrunched them tighter shut. Confused images flitted through my mind – hounds with red eyes and fangs . . . sharp stabbing beaks. Why hadn't I listened to Gabe?

'Not so nice when you're on the receiving end, is it?'

I looked up to see Matt standing above me, Jez barking at his side. She seemed pleased to see him, but if I could have got up and decked him, I would have. As it was, I just glared.

'I knew you'd come back,' I said. I was trying for cool, but it's kind of difficult when you're lying on the ground like a sack of potatoes.

'Yeah, yeah. But I nearly didn't. So what's wrong?'

'Obvious, isn't it?' I pointed to my hiking sock. 'And it's all your stupid fault.'

I have to say it for Matt – he was quite good about the situation. He didn't apologise for making me fall over, but he found a stick for me to lean on and chucked it over to me. When he saw I was having difficulty, he put on this bored face but came over and helped me to my feet. To be honest, my ankle wasn't that bad any more, but I milked it for all it was worth. Then I remembered the thing at the bottom of the standing stone and poked the ground with my stick. It gave a faint metallic dink.

Matt frowned. 'What's that?'

'Don't know. Buried treasure?'

Matt snorted. 'The devil's crusty old toenail, more like.'

But he bent down and started fumbling in the leaf mould anyway. Jez tried to join in but he pushed her aside – gently, though. Maybe he was beginning to like her after all.

'It's some sort of box,' he said, and tugged at it impatiently.

'Let me,' I said. 'I'm the one who found it.'

I shoved him aside and tried to reach down to it, but my ankle made me yelp with pain. Matt sighed, helped me up again and knelt down at the foot of the standing stone. When tugging at the box didn't work, he dug carefully around its sides until it shifted. At last he pulled it out. It was made of blackened metal, about the length of a paperback but much narrower, with a rusty catch at the side. He stood and, after a moment's hesitation, handed it to me. It wasn't heavy – no gold coins, then. I brushed the leaf mould off it, jiggled the catch and prised open the lid.

Inside, lying on a bed of folded purple velvet, was a skull. A tiny white head with a long, thin, curving bill. It took me a minute to realise that this was the skull of a bird, and not some mutant animal or baby dinosaur. The bill was huge – totally out of proportion to the head.

Balancing on my stick, I turned away from Matt

and picked the skull out of the box. It was as light as a feather. And it belonged to me. I didn't want to show Matt.

'What are you doing?' he said, reaching round and grabbing at my hand. 'Give it to me. I want to see it, too.' He sounded angry. His voice was different – harder.

'Careful!' I said. 'You'll break it, you clumsy idiot!' But I handed over the skull, even though I didn't want to.

Matt held it in both hands and stared at it. 'What do you think it is?' he whispered.

I found myself whispering, too. 'A wading bird. Like a curlew or a whimbrel. That beak's for digging things out of the mud. But you don't get waders in the middle of a wood. It's all wrong.'

'Why? It didn't fly into the box all on its own, did it?' said Matt, louder now. He was acting confident, but it wasn't that convincing.

I took out the purple material from the bottom of the box. It was faded and worn, with a kind of raised pattern of velvet leaves. It reminded me of something, I couldn't think what.

'So how did it get here then, if you're so clever?' I said.

'I don't know. But I think we should put it back.'

I was so surprised I wobbled on my ankle and nearly fell over again.

'No way,' I said. 'You can't mean that. I'm keeping it.'

Matt hesitated. 'Listen a minute, will you? Gabe warned me about something last night.' He rubbed his nose, embarrassed, but ploughed on. 'He said there would be omens. Birds first – they're the harbingers, he said, though I don't know what of. The thing is, couldn't this be one of them?'

I rolled my eyes. Why was he acting like such a moron?

'Gabe's completely loopy. And you are, too, if you believe what he says.'

'Fine. Have it your own way. I don't care if something awful happens.'

'Yeah, well. So long as it gets you out of our hair.'

Matt glared at me. Then he took the velvet from me, put it back in the box and placed the skull on top.

'What is it with you?' he said. 'You've been horrible ever since I arrived. What have I ever done to you?'

'Do you *really* not know?' I said. My body was suddenly rigid with anger. 'The farm, that's what. Grandad left it to Mum, but he left half to Aunty

Caroline, too. Only she doesn't want to keep her share – she just wants the money. She's been asking for ages. And now she's getting divorced from your dad, she says she really needs the whole lot. Which means we might have to sell the farm, even though she has her own house and it's a lot bigger than ours. The greedy cow.'

Matt was breathing hard and his cheekbones flushed red. The rest of his face was totally white. He looked like he wanted to thump me.

I took a step backwards. 'I can't believe you had the nerve to come and stay,' I said. 'But then, you were dumped, weren't you? Dumped by your dad, dumped by your mum, and now you're dumped on us.'

Matt made a grab for me. I sidestepped too fast on to my bad ankle and cried out in pain. Above us a bird whistled, high and clear and long. Then a whole load of them rose out of the trees, cackling and screaming.

Suddenly I felt shaky. We both gazed down at the skull. I couldn't hear birds any more, just the rushing of the stream merging with the rushing in my head. A shadow spread over the clearing.

'I'm out of here,' said Matt. Although he still looked pale, his mouth was set in a determined line. He snapped the lid of the box shut. I could see his fingers trembling slightly, but I didn't say anything. The only thing that mattered now was getting home.

Matt stuffed the box into my rucksack and slung it over his shoulder.

'Come on, Jez,' he said, and she trotted to his side, the traitor. He stroked her black fur like she was an old friend – and she let him. I shot her a baleful look. Then I found the path and limped out of Old Scratch Wood, and on to the waiting moor.

7

Matt

I was so glad to get out of there. Even with that little cow Tilda hobbling in front of me, barely saying a word. I wished I'd left her in the middle of the wood. That mask thing she pulled on me was bad enough, but finding the freaky bird skull was even worse. It made my skin crawl just to think about it. Yet somehow I didn't want to hand it over to Tilda. I could feel the box banging against my back with every step.

We walked for ages and ages in silence. The route across the moor was unbelievably barren and depressing, and it was getting windier, too. The sun was lowering and lowering in the sky. Soon it would be dusk. I wished Tilda would get a move on, but her ankle was really slowing us up.

I tried to forget Gabe's talk about omens, but I couldn't stop it sidling into my mind. *Watching, waiting*, he'd said. *Get away from here as fast as you can, before you bring on something worse*. No wonder all those birds shrieking their heads off in the middle of that foul wood had made me so jumpy. My heart was still thumping away.

The dark moorland stretched out around us. How anyone could like it was beyond me. It was better than being in the middle of Old Scratch Wood, but only just. At least out here we'd be able to see whatever was creeping up on us, I supposed. And we had Jez – I reckoned she'd be able to see off most things. But I couldn't wait to get back. OK, the farmhouse wasn't up to much, but with luck Uncle Jack would have lit a fire and it wouldn't be quite so miserable.

Time to think about something else. I concentrated hard on what Tilda had said back there about the farm, and Mum wanting to sell her half. So that was what had been getting up her nose all this time. It was news to me. But actually . . . quite good news. It would be even better if Mum decided to hand some of the money to me. That would be really great. I'd buy my own boat and sail around the world. Maybe life was looking up after all . . . but I knew better than to say that to Tilda.

I should try to smooth things over, I decided.

'I never knew about the farm, you know,' I said. 'Mum owning part of it, I mean.'

She turned and stared at me. Her red hair crackled with electricity.

'Then you're even more stupid than you look,' she said. 'We sold off three fields just before Mum died because Aunty Caroline said she needed the money. Mum was furious. She couldn't believe her sister would do that to her. It's so selfish.'

I blinked but forced myself not to react. Poisonous little toad.

It was interesting, though. That must have been, what, around three years ago? When Dad spent so much money doing up the boat, and he and Mum were fighting all the time. But I'd have thought Aunty Rose would have been happy to help her sister out. I mean, what do a few fields matter?

'What do a few fields matter?' I said.

Tilda looked as if she might combust. She swivelled round on her stick and virtually spat at me.

'You keep a farm together, whatever happens. If you

knew anything, you'd know that – it's been in the family long enough. You don't sell it off in dribs and drabs until you're left with all the worst pasture and you can't make enough money to keep it running and it gets so weak it finally dies. Though I suppose your mum'll make sure she takes her full share well before then.'

'Oh, get off your high horse,' I said. 'That's not going to happen for ages, is it? And you'll be off somewhere else by then. Let's face it, no one would want to stick around here.'

Tilda's face was as red as her hair now. '*I* would!' she yelled. 'You just don't get it, do you? This is my home.'

She forged ahead through the dead bracken, almost forgetting to limp. Jez followed her, tail down, her whole body looking like a reproach. I wished I was somewhere else, somewhere warm and welcoming and ordinary.

It was then I remembered Paul. His arm round my mum's waist. His pathetic attempts to be nice to me. Yes, Tilda might end up losing her stupid farm. But I was losing my family. Everything that was precious to me was going totally pear-shaped – Mum and Dad breaking up, Paul moving into our house, me thinking I was escaping by coming here, my toxic cousin making my stay a misery. I should be at home watching *Avatar* with a big bowl of crisps in front of me instead of being stuck here. It was all Paul's fault. I hated his guts.

I wasn't going to take it any more. There had to be a way to wipe that smarmy smile off his face, to make Mum see sense so she'd kick him out of our house and Dad could come home.

I walked faster and stuck my hands in my pockets to keep them warm, but it didn't have much effect. Then I thought of the food Tilda had brought. I was starving. I opened the top of the rucksack and rummaged about. My frozen fingers closed around the box containing the skull, and I jerked my hand away quickly.

We'd passed Thieves' Tor now. Ahead of us was the road, with the farm track leading off it. Fields stretched out on either side of the track, green against the brown of the moorland we'd come from. There in the hollow was the farm and all its huddled buildings. At last.

It was really bitter now, though. I put my hood up as I crossed the road on to the farm track so the wind didn't make my head hurt quite so much. That's why I didn't hear the screeching straight away. Black shapes were rising at the corner of Far Field. Crows, I thought vaguely. Why were there so many?

Suddenly Tilda started hurtling down the farm track, then up the ridge, her stick thumping away at top speed. For a minute I stood there watching her, then I started running too, Jez racing alongside me.

'What is it?' I yelled. The wind whipped my words away and sent them whistling in all directions. Tilda didn't stop.

We were on it now: a white shape lying by the hedge. Its middle was a raw-red pulpy mess. A crow fluttered up from it, barely bothered by our arrival. Something pink and stringy hung from the side of its beak. As we came closer I could see the shape was a sheep. It lay on its side, twitching its legs pathetically. Where there should have been an eye was a dark, bloody socket. The air smelt of iron.

Tilda looked as if she'd been punched in the face.

'What can we do?' I said.

'Nothing.'

'There must be *something*.' I couldn't bear it. I'd never seen anything so horrible.

She shook her head. 'Put her out of her misery, that's all. They've started on her insides – she doesn't have a chance. I'm going to get Dad.'

I turned away from the ewe and her empty eye. She wasn't even bleating. Just lying there, taking it. She'd given up. All the other sheep just went on munching the grass as if nothing had happened.

Tilda sped off towards the farm. I followed with Jez, feeling sick. As we made our way down the ridge, more crows flapped over to the sheep.

Uncle Jack brought his gun but he didn't need it. The ewe had gone. Died, I mean, not disappeared. He slung her over his shoulders to take her down to the farm. It reminded me of those pictures from Bible stories. A Jesus pose. But not a happy one. Not happy at all.

8

Kitty

Daddy brought back one of our sheep but it's all dead now. He says it hurt its leg and the crows killed it and that's two lambs we won't be having in the spring. I wanted to look but he wouldn't let me. Tilda hurt her leg, too. She's very cross. Her and Matt found a bird head in the wood. It's white with great big holes for its eyes and a big long beak. I was allowed to hold it just for a minute only Tilda said I had to put it down or I might break it. I'm watching it, though. It's funny. The end of its beak is going all black.

9

Matt

I kept waking up in the night, convinced I was back in the middle of Old Scratch Wood and that Paul was there, too, laughing at me. It took me till about five to fall asleep properly, and it felt like only minutes later that I became aware of something clawing at the bedclothes – sharp and vicious and insistent. I burrowed deeper underneath the cover, but something plucked it back from my face. A black-beaked shape from out of my sleep slowly morphed into the silhouette of Tilda, her red hair backlit by the light that shimmered through the curtains.

'Get up,' she said, and tugged at the sheet again. 'Slob.'

'What time is it?' I mumbled.

'Quarter past seven. The animals need feeding, so get a move on.'

I groaned. She couldn't be serious.

Unfortunately, she was. In fact she seemed determined to make my life a misery. She switched on the lamp next to me and I had to scrunch my eyes up to get away from the glare.

'Are you actually going to help around here or just sponge off us all the time?'

I wasn't going to let her score any more points off me. 'Five minutes,' I said furiously. 'But only if you get out of my room right now.'

She banged the door. I threw on some clothes and stumbled downstairs. I'd intended to look at the skull again – it was nagging at my mind – but Tilda was already at the front door putting on her wellies.

'How's the leg?' I said. 'Had a miraculous recovery, then?'

Tilda pulled a face. 'It still hurts. But I can walk – no thanks to you.' She limped out in this really obvious way. What a drama queen.

I caught up with her in the back yard. She'd already fed the overgrown puppies, which were running round in circles as if they were possessed. One of them jumped up at me, leaving great muddy footprints all over my jacket.

'Down, Lawless!' said Tilda. But I could see her smirk as she scattered corn for the chickens.

'What have you done with the skull?' I said. 'I want another look at it.'

'Nothing. And it's mine, by the way. So you won't be seeing it any time soon.'

I glared at her, but she was busy putting fresh water in the chickens' drinkers and didn't even notice.

'So what am I supposed to do round here, then?' I said, brushing the dirt off my jacket.

'Go and let the geese out. They're in the side yard through there – the barn with the blue door. And give them this.' She shoved a bucketful of pellets at me.

I opened the gate. The side yard was half taken up by a mucky-looking pond that must belong to the geese. I found the blue door and lifted its wooden latch. Instantly I took a step back.

Long white necks were snaking towards me and the sound of hissing rose into the air, loud and alarming. Suddenly the geese were all around me: ten or twelve of them, huge white birds with bright orange beaks, all of them waving their necks at me and sticking out their tongues like a pit full of angry cobras. One flapped its enormous wings at me as if to let me know it meant business. Then a beak snapped towards my hand. I jumped backwards but they kept on coming, charging towards me, hissing and swaying.

I dropped the bucket and ran.

Tilda wasn't with the chickens any more. I found her in the front yard outside East Barn. By then I was so angry I could hardly get the words out.

'You knew they'd do that, didn't you?' I said.

She grinned unpleasantly. 'Hungry, were they? What have you done with the bucket?'

'Get it yourself. I'm going in for some breakfast.'

'Oh, don't be so pathetic, Matt,' she said. 'It was a joke, that's all. Look, you can carry on sulking, or you can come and see the calf that's been put in East Barn. Dad brought in one of the cows yesterday because there's something wrong with her foot, and her calf had to come, too. It was born in May but it's not weaned yet. But hey, don't strain yourself. It's not like you'll be able to do anything remotely useful.'

I considered going straight back into the house, hunting out the skull from wherever Tilda had put it, and hiding it so she'd never ever find it again. Instead I found myself following her into the barn. And the calf *was* sweet, with its great big eyes. Until its mother decided to go completely mental, that was.

It happened so quickly. Tilda had got inside the pen and was cooing at the calf. She looked back at me with a nasty smile on her face, as if she was about to give me another job I'd hate. Behind her I could see this enormous great cow moving towards its calf. Its nostrils flared dangerously.

I was about to say something, I honestly was. Only I was too late. All at once the cow was pinning Tilda's arm against the bar of the pen, leaning on it and snorting and stamping its feet. It looked as if it was about to have a fit. Tilda screamed, her arm and shoulder jammed against the bar.

I leant over and pushed the cow tentatively, but it was like pushing a mountain. Tilda screamed again, a scream full of pain. This time I didn't stop to think. I picked up a broom and just whacked the cow over the side with it. It let out this long mournful moo, but didn't shift an inch.

'Quick!' Tilda yelled. 'Hit it!'

I whacked the cow again, harder this time. It bellowed blue murder. Then, very, very slowly, it shuffled away and started nuzzling its calf.

Tilda darted out of the gate and banged it shut. She clutched her arm, tears rolling down her face. Not surprising really – a cow must weigh half a tonne. You don't want that crushing the life out of you.

'Are you OK?' I said. I was worried the thing might have dislocated her shoulder.

Tilda wiped her cheeks and tentatively shook her arm. Then she managed a weak smile.

'Yeah,' she said. 'All in one piece still. She didn't put all her weight against me.' She looked at me for a second, then her eyes shifted away. 'Thanks,' she said, quickly.

'So what was that about?' I said, glancing at the cow. It looked totally calm now, feeding its calf and looking about as vicious as a telephone directory.

'It was my fault,' said Tilda. 'You shouldn't get between a cow and its calf. I was really stupid.'

Was that all? I wondered. My mind flicked to the curlew skull with its tiny, delicate head and gigantic curved beak. 'Maybe something else was freaking her out, too,' I said. 'Same with the geese. It's like they've been spooked.'

Tilda rolled her eyes. 'Geese are always like that,' she said. 'That's why I got you to let them out. And I told you, it was my fault with the cow. You're sounding just like Gabe.'

'He was right about the birds, though,' I said. 'And

it could be that we found one of his omens. Buried in that box.'

'Oooh, really, really scary,' said Tilda in a stupid high-pitched voice. 'Gabe doesn't know the first thing about anything. Anyway, I got Dad to look at the skull last night. He said it probably *is* a curlew, so I was right. And even if it was one of Gabe's stupid birds, maybe you hadn't noticed that it's kind of dead?'

I gave up. I knew perfectly well that she'd been as freaked as me when everything had kicked off with the skull, but now she was making me out to be a complete idiot for taking any of it seriously. But if I hadn't been there, what might that cow have done? I'd had enough of Tilda this morning. I headed indoors.

Uncle Jack was in the living room, bent over his ancient computer doing what looked like farm accounts. He barely even looked up. Tilda got a better reception when she came in. Kitty leapt on her immediately and dragged her off to sort out a costume for Hallowe'en – it was at the end of the week and she was going to be a skeleton, only she was determined to wear a pink tutu as well. I clearly wasn't wanted.

I loafed about the kitchen for a bit, filling up on cereal and wondering what to do with myself. The skull wasn't anywhere to be seen. Tilda must have stashed it away in her room. Finally Uncle Jack appeared, on the hunt for coffee.

'I thought Tilda was in here,' he said. I shrugged. He turned and looked at me. 'Getting on, are you?'

I didn't say anything. He raked a hand through his unkempt hair, looked closely at me for a second or two, then sighed.

'Too bad you had to find that ewe yesterday,' he said. 'It's a real shame. She was one of my better beasts. Can't be helped, though.'

I wondered whether to mention the cow, but Uncle Jack looked so fed up I didn't like to. Abruptly he changed the subject.

'Couldn't sleep last night for some reason, so I looked up your find from yesterday in one of Rose's bird books,' he said. 'She had a lot of those.' For a minute he seemed very far away. 'Anyway, it's a curlew all right. Not making much noise now, your one, but in the wild, curlews have a really haunting cry – a kind of whistling sound. Apparently, sailors see them as a bad omen – I suppose it's because they sound a bit like a storm. Very superstitious bunch, sailors.' He suddenly scratched his beard, embarrassed. 'Though I'm sure your dad isn't, Matthew. Or you, for that matter. I gather you're pretty good on the helm yourself.'

'Actually Dad *is* a bit superstitious,' I said. 'It's Mum who says she doesn't believe in stuff like that. But I'm not sure that's true. She never wants to come here . . .' My voice trailed off.

Tilda was standing by the door, her shoulders rigid.

'Now, that reminds me,' said Uncle Jack, glancing between the two of us, 'your mum called again this morning. She wants you to ring back – says you haven't spoken to her since you've been here. I assured her you were still in the land of the living. But give her a call, Matt, won't you? Use the landline. And I'd better get back to the fencing. There's another gap up in Far Field and if I don't sort it soon, the sheep'll be out.'

I ignored Tilda and went off to make the call. Next to the phone on the old wooden sideboard in the hall was a picture I hadn't spotted before – Mum and Aunty Rose when they were young, in matching dark dresses. Aunty Rose looked really sulky. Mum had an arm round her and was staring straight ahead with a sort of anxious smile. I could tell she was unhappy about something.

To be honest, I was missing her, even though I'd been so furious with her when I first came here. Maybe she'd have realised how wrong she'd been about letting Paul stay. Maybe she'd even be ready to take Dad back by now.

I should have known. Paul answered, sounding like he owned the place.

'Matt, at long last,' he said. 'Excellent, excellent. Your mother's been worried about you.'

I bristled. If Paul weren't there, she wouldn't have to worry about me. And with him living in our house, Dad was never going to come back.

'Hope the moor's treating you well?'

'Suppose so.'

'Marvellous. Marvellous.'

Why does he always have to say everything twice? It's bad enough having to listen to him once. Anyway, he'd obviously decided he wasn't going to get much out of me. He called Mum over and got off the phone fast.

Mum quizzed me about the farm and Uncle Jack and the girls, but even though I was bursting to, I didn't let on about how nasty Tilda's been or how creepy the place is. The last thing I want is for Mum to come and fetch me. Dad won't be back for at least two weeks, and there's no way I can stand living at home with Paul there for that amount of time. Soon Mum was wittering on about some fancy dinner they'd been to. I made an excuse and said goodbye.

Kitty trotted into the hall in her skeleton suit and tutu.

'Matt, will you come and look for eggs with me?' she asked. 'There might be blue ones.' She took my hand and pulled.

'Do I have a choice?' I said, but I knew it was no use. Kitty was a force of nature. Besides, there was something seriously nice about her all-out friendliness.

The chickens were pleased to see us, too. They zoomed up, all legs and outsize feet and swaying, armless bodies, looking ridiculous.

'Hello, chickies. Hello, Bella. Hello, Mabel. Hello, Elvis,' said Kitty.

I wasn't so sure about the cockerel – the spurs on the inside of his feet were about three inches long and dangerous-looking, and he had to lift his legs over them each time he took a step. But Kitty wasn't fazed. She marched straight over to the laying boxes at the back of the shed.

There was a whole clutch of eggs, and yes, two of them were bluish green. Kitty loaded them into her basket as if they were made of gold. I felt my spirits lift, then plummet again as I spotted Gabe edging towards us. His black beanie was pulled right down over his eyebrows.

'Hello, Gabe,' Kitty said, and threw him a drop-dead gorgeous smile. Even he was a pushover when it came to Kitty. It was like he'd had a total character transplant.

'Hello there, young lady. I like your outfit. How are those chickies of yours doing, then?'

'They're very well, thank you. They've laid six eggs today.'

Gabe nodded. 'Not too bad,' he said. 'Now if you run on inside directly, young Kitty, you'll find a lemon drizzle cake Alba baked last night.'

Kitty shot off like a greyhound after a rabbit. With a sinking feeling I realised that Gabe had got her out of the way in order to have another of his little chats with me. He sat down on a straw bale and motioned me to do the same. For a moment he stared at me again. His eyes were deep-set and the palest of blues. Probably centuries of inbreeding, I thought, but banished the idea fast, wondering if he could read my mind.

'OK, Matt Crimmond,' he said. 'Tilda doesn't listen to me, so you'd better. Because I know what's going on. I've been around nearly sixty years and I can read the signs.' He waggled a filthy finger in my direction.

'What signs?' I said.

'There's bad blood between you and Tilda,' he said. 'I can see it. And that means bad things can come to you. What happened in Old Scratch Wood?'

I caught my breath. 'I didn't see anything,' I said. 'Well, not anything that matters.' I wasn't going to mention the curlew skull, that was for sure. I'd had enough of people making fun of me.

Gabe smiled, but it wasn't a friendly smile.

'Nothing?' he said. 'No birds acting strange, then? No animals?'

'Nothing,' I said. 'Nothing at all.'

'That ewe with its eye pecked out – you just think on that,' said Gabe. 'That was proper nasty. And Tilda's just told me about her run-in with the cow out there. I told you already – the harbingers are gathering. And I think you know it now.'

I didn't want him to see how rattled I was. 'I've no idea what you're on about,' I said. 'Those are just random things. And yeah, Tilda had her arm trapped against the pen. But she got in the way of the calf – she was stupid. She said so.'

Gabe frowned, his face creasing up into hundreds of tiny lines.

'Animals can tell when there's evil on the loose,' he said. 'They sense it way before us folk. They know when fire's coming or the earth's shaking. And they know when the gabbleratchet stirs.'

He shut up suddenly and picked up a petrol can from beside the straw bales. 'Right. I'll be going. I need to sort the tractor.'

'Wait,' I said. 'The gabbleratchet? Wasn't that what you said before? What is it? Tell me.'

Gabe's eyes slid away.

'Best you don't know,' he said. 'Maybe we'll be spared. This time.'

I was beginning to get annoyed now. Part of me wondered if he was hamming it up for my benefit. You know, let's scare the townie for a laugh.

'Sounds like rubbish to me,' I said.

Gabe looked thunderous. 'You listen here now, boy,' he said. 'The harbingers – the birds – they're sent out to test you. You might just be able to turn them back. But the gabbleratchet – that's different. It's a curse. If it comes, make sure you don't look at it. Get away from it as quick as you can and forget you ever heard it. Because if you see it, a death follows close after.'

'But what is it? How will I know not to look at it if you don't tell me what it is?'

He was silent for a moment. Then he cleared his throat.

'Listen out for the geese,' he said.

My skin began to prickle. 'What, the geese on the farm?'

'Not them, boy. Wild geese, isn't it? Whistling through the skies on stormy nights. That's how it starts. Or so they say.'

I made an effort to relax my shoulders again, but I couldn't help thinking about the geese I'd seen over the tor on my first night here.

'Geese, right,' I said. 'And then what?'

Gabe just shook his head. 'Like I said. Best you don't know.'

He glanced at me. I tried to hide how anxious I felt.

'It's no use smiling, boy,' he said. 'These things have a way of being true whether you believe in them or not.'

10

Tilda

It had been lashing down all afternoon – the kind of freezing Dartmoor rain that doesn't let up for hours. I lay on my bed listening to it hammering away on the corrugated iron of the tractor shed. I like the rain most of the time, but with any luck it would be driving Matt crazy.

Last night I'd left the skull in its box and hidden it under my bed. I'd held off opening it up again, although I'd hardly stopped thinking about it ever since we found it. Now I got off the bed, took it out and placed it on my desk. It stared at me from hollow eye sockets. I was struck again by how beautiful and strange it was. I had to admit there was something kind of cruel about it, but that didn't bother me – it was totally brilliant. And it belonged to me. After all, I'd figured out what it was. City boy didn't have the faintest – left to himself he'd probably have thought it was a flamingo.

The skull would look good on my dressing table, if I could make a space for it. I love stuff like that, stones and fossils and crystals. I'm always finding interesting things on the moor and bringing them back – feathers, owl pellets, adder skins. Once I even found a dead mole. That one didn't last long. Mum made me bury it straight away, which wasn't really fair, since it wasn't like it was festering or anything – it was all soft and glossy. Dad says my room looks like the Natural History Museum, but that doesn't bother me. I think it's cool.

I flopped back on my bed and gazed at my new find. There was no way I was sharing it with Matt. Why should I, when he just wanted to get his hands on everything we owned? He shouldn't be here at all, not with the farm going up for sale whenever his mum says the word. It was horrible. He and his mother were going to ruin everything. They were going to take away everything that reminded me of *my* mum. And at some point I'd make sure Matt paid for that.

I got up again and went across to the skull. The weird thing was that it seemed a bit different today. I'm sure I remembered it just being black towards its tip. Now most of the beak was black, and it felt somehow heavier than before. Obviously my mind was playing tricks on me.

Anyway, I needed to get the supper on. I'd promised Dad we'd do it today as he was going to be busy. Matt was in his room – he's good at avoiding work – but Kitty came down to the kitchen to keep me company.

'Do you want to see my picture?' she said, thrusting a drawing at me. As per usual it wasn't very obvious what it might be. Some kind of crazily coloured animals, that much I could guess.

'Are those our calves?' I said, pointing at some black squiggles with four legs.

'No, they're dogs, silly,' said Kitty. 'And these green ones are birdies.'

I congratulated her on her artistic ability and got her to set the table. I even let her pour honey all over the chicken drumsticks, which was a really bad idea because she refused to stop and nearly used up the whole jar. Oh, well. Supper would be extra sticky tonight. I didn't suppose it would matter much.

It was only when Dad came in from the fields with

Jez, both of them soaked to the skin, that Matt finally showed up. He just expects to be fed – he doesn't seem to realise that it has to be cooked first. It's like he hasn't even noticed that Mum's not here any more. Anyway, Dad changed quickly, and we all sat down and tore into supper. Honey chicken, potatoes, carrots and broccoli. For a while there was nothing but contented chomping. Dad finally put his fork down and told me how good it was.

'I helped,' said Kitty.

'And you're a very good cook, too. There's no stinting on the honey with you.'

All through the chitter-chatter you could see Matt was squirming to say something. Finally he turned to Dad.

'Uncle Jack, have you ever heard of the gabble-ratchet?'

I frowned. Wasn't that the thing Gabe had mentioned? How come Matt suddenly knew all about it?

'Can't say I have,' said Dad. I thought he'd leave it at that – he hasn't been talking much to Matt, which is totally fair enough. But Dad can't resist a story.

'Do you know what it is?' he said.

To my annoyance, Matt had one up on me. He told

us what Gabe had been spouting to him – that at the beginning it sounds like a load of geese flying over and honking. Big deal.

'I seem to remember something about that legend,' said Dad. 'Geese turning into something else – and if you see it, hideous things will happen to you. Maybe the gabbleratchet's another word for it.' He glanced at Kitty. 'OK, darling, you can get down now.' He waited till she'd disappeared.

'So,' he said. 'From what I remember, the story they tell here is that wild geese are the devil's servants. And when they change, they become a pack of demonic creatures charging across the moor. Hunting. Get in their way and you're doomed.'

Matt was silent for a moment. He takes all this supernatural stuff way too seriously. Then he started up again.

'Old Scratch is another name for the devil, isn't it? So has the gabbleratchet got anything to do with Old Scratch Wood?'

Dad shrugged. 'There are loads of places on Dartmoor with a connection to the devil. All I know is that anyone unlucky enough to find themselves in the path of these creatures would be cursed. They'd go home and find someone in their family had died. Or they'd be chased over a cliff and smashed to pieces. That's what the folk tales say, anyway.'

'You sound as bad as Gabe,' I said, crossly. I don't like it when Dad tries to scare me about the moor.

None of us had noticed Kitty slip back in from the living room. Suddenly she made her presence felt.

'Gabbleratchet,' she said. 'Gabbleratchet. Gabble-ratchet. Gabbleratchet.' She was shouting now. 'Gabbleratchet! Gabbleratchet! Gabbleratchet!' She started running in circles round the table, yelling and whooping.

The word was pulsating in my ears. Kitty often gets over-excited about stuff, but this time it was freaking me out. Matt looked totally horrified, and even Dad seemed a bit pained.

'Enough!' I shouted. I grabbed her and held on. 'Bedtime for you!'

'Not going to bed,' Kitty said, struggling.

'Shush,' I said. 'No more arguments.'

I frogmarched her upstairs, did her teeth and a quick wash and got her into her bunny pyjamas. I sat with her for a while, reading her favourite book, but she wasn't really listening. Finally I put the light out.

'Is the gabbleratchet coming, Tilda?' she murmured.

'Don't be silly,' I said. 'Of course not. There's no

such thing.'

I shut the door softly and crept away.

When I came down again, Dad was sprawled in his usual place on the sofa and Matt was nowhere to be seen. Good, I thought. I'd been wanting to get Dad on his own – I really needed to talk to him. He gave me the perfect lead-in.

'Is Matt behaving himself, then?' he said. 'Helping out a bit?'

I laughed, but it came out more like a strangled cough that made Jez jump.

'What do *you* think? Why do we have to have him, Dad?'

He sighed. 'You know perfectly well. Come on, Tilda, you do realise his family's going through a really hard time, don't you?'

'Oh, like we haven't been? Not that Matt seems to have noticed.'

Dad sat up and patted the spot next to him.

'Darling, I know how difficult it's been for you since your mum died. You've coped brilliantly. Sometimes I worry about how much you do round the house. And I know how much you miss her.'

I turned my head so he wouldn't see my eyes getting wet.

'I'm fine,' I said.

'Good girl. Anyway, with his dad away, I gather Matt's finding it hard to adjust to the changes.'

'You mean Aunty Caroline's new boyfriend?'

'Yes. Some banker type, apparently. Matt's taking it badly. Just try to cut him a bit of slack. The boy's suffering.'

'Well, so what?' I said. I felt all my pent-up fury rise to the surface like an ash cloud. 'I don't see why we should put up with him when he's going to take the farm away from us. We don't need anyone else here. We're fine, just you, me and Kitty. We shouldn't even be talking to him, let alone feeding him. It's like offering your supper to a cannibal.'

Dad turned and faced me.

'You've got to get over this, Tilda,' he said. 'Matt's your cousin. I know your mum and her sister didn't always see eye to eye, with Caroline being such a city girl at heart. But Caroline can't help the fact that she inherited half the farm and doesn't care for farming. What would you expect your grandfather to do? Just give it to your mum? That would be like me leaving everything to Kitty and nothing to you. It wouldn't be fair, would it?'

I scowled. 'Yeah, well, Aunty Caroline's not much

of a sister, is she?'

'Tilda!' Dad sounded really shocked. 'Your mum loved her, even if they didn't see each other that much. Just remember, this farm business isn't Caroline's fault. And it's certainly not Matt's. Anyway, you never know.' He broke into a grin. 'After a few days here he might find himself wanting to be a farmer. So stick with it, Tilda. It might all come out right in the end.'

'Yeah, like that'll happen,' I said. 'Matt hates the country. He hates everything about Dartmoor. And even if he didn't, I wouldn't share anything with him. I'd honestly rather the farm was sold.'

Dad looked at me and frowned. I shut up. There was no point in going on at him, but I wasn't giving up that easily. If Matt thought he was suffering now, he didn't know the half of it. For some reason the skull floated into my head, and suddenly I knew how I could get back at him. And this was a whole lot better than a stupid werewolf mask.

I trailed back upstairs to my room. This time I knew I wasn't imagining it. The curlew skull was definitely different – the beak was nearly all black. It wasn't as long as I remembered either – somehow it looked wider, blunter. It must be some weird microbe thing going on.

I was just about to pick it up when my bedroom door opened. Matt pushed it wide and came straight in without even knocking.

'Let's have a look at it, then,' he said. 'I knew you had it in here.'

'What are you doing in my room?' I said. 'It's private!'

'Yeah, well, we both found the skull, so it belongs to both of us,' said Matt.

'*I* found it! Just get out!' I was furious. And for some reason I didn't want him touching the skull. I picked it up and held it tight.

'Keep your hair on. You could try being nice. After all, we *are* family.'

'Some family,' I said. I could feel my blood rushing to my head. I knew I was shouting, but I couldn't stop. 'You're going to break up everything that Mum and Dad worked for here. You and your precious mum.'

Matt gaped at me.

'It's not like she needs her part of the farm anyway. And now she's got this rich banker boyfriend, too, so she needs it even less. Hey, maybe they'll sell *your* house and buy a great big new one together and you'll have to leave your school and all your friends. Just like I will if we lose the farm.'

I'd really riled him now. I figured I might as well put the final nail in the coffin. The thing that had come to me when Dad was telling me off. The one thing that was really going to hurt him.

'Or maybe they'll send you away, so they can be alone together. Because now she's found Paul, your mum won't want you any more, Matt. Just like your dad doesn't.'

Matt's mouth had fallen open. He took a step towards me, clenching his fists.

'Just stop it,' he said. It came out fierce and cold. 'Just stop it now. You're a nasty, jealous, evil . . .'

Matt's chest rose and fell. I was sure that he wanted to hit me and was only just managing to hold himself back. I felt the air go out of me.

'Don't you ever talk about my mother again, do you hear?' he said. His words were like hammer blows. 'I mean it. Or else.'

He stormed out and banged the door after him. I picked up the skull and held it in my palm. My hand was shaking, but only a bit, and the skull was satisfyingly heavy. Matt could rant all he liked. I didn't care.

11

Matt

I slept in really late the next day. Tilda didn't bother waking me up. Good thing, too – I was still seething from last night, and the more I thought about it, the angrier I felt. I'd had enough now – there was no way I was going to spend another day under the same roof as my cousin. I just couldn't believe she'd come out with that about Mum. If she was a boy I'd have thumped her there and then. I had to get out of here before I exploded.

Her and her stupid farm. If it was up to me, I'd sell the whole thing tomorrow.

And it wasn't just about Tilda. Gabe's mad warnings about curses and animals going weird had really got to me. I was so jumpy now that I'd started imagining all sorts of crazy things. I wasn't overjoyed at the thought of going home, though. Paul would be all over me like a rash, thinking I'd forgiven him and that everything was suddenly sweetness and light. I wasn't putting myself through that. Anyway, it was all because of him and Mum that I'd come to this hole in the first place. It would serve them right if I didn't come back at all.

I stuffed my things into my bag. It took about three seconds flat as I didn't bother to fold anything. I took down Dad's burgee last and threw that in, too. Then I opened my bedroom door a fraction. Not a sound. The coast was clear.

As quietly as I could, I crept across the corridor to Tilda's room and stood outside, listening. I eased the door open. No one there. The skull was sitting on her dressing table, looking stranger than ever. I could even see its metal box on top of an untidy pile of clothes beside her bed. Perfect. I took a deep breath, then went in and grabbed it, packing it away inside the box. I didn't know why I was taking it with me – it wasn't as if I even liked the thing. In fact I found it sort of repulsive. But Tilda was in love with it. That would teach her.

It wasn't till I got to the farm gate that I started breathing normally. No one had even noticed that I'd gone. And let's face it, if Tilda had spotted me with my luggage, she'd probably be halfway through a victory dance before I reached the front door.

I went down the farm track, skirting Long Field and hoping I wouldn't meet Uncle Jack. But no one appeared. The sheep over in Far Field all looked happy enough today, but I knew now what the whole nature thing was really like.

I had a rough idea which way Widecombe was, and I figured I could pick up a bus from there, or failing that, a taxi or a lift, or anything that was going, so long as it would take me off the moor. It was well past three now and I hoped I wasn't too late. But something would turn up, I was sure.

I turned right at the end of the farm track where we'd crossed over on to the moor yesterday. Dry stone walls ran along the road on either side, and beyond them, fields dotted with more sheep. I concentrated on putting one foot in front of the other and clearing my mind of all its nagging thoughts. Left. Right. Left. Right. Nothing else mattered. I hoped I'd be able to find the way. No signposts, of course. That would obviously be far too much to expect out here in the land that time forgot. There wasn't any traffic either. Just the grey sky and the fields stretching out, and beyond them the brown moorland with its scattered fingers of tors.

In minutes I was a bit calmer. There was something about just being on my own and taking it all in through my eyes and my lungs that made me feel – I don't know – sort of at one with my surroundings. *Hey, steady on*, I thought. You don't want to start acting like some country bumpkin just when you're getting out of here. That would be really sad. Think of something else. All the tube stations on the Piccadilly line, for starters.

I was only at King's Cross when I heard my name being called. I looked up and felt my chest go tight. It was Gabe, and he was rushing down the road towards me.

'Where do you think you're going now, Matt Crimmond?' he shouted.

I stopped dead and waited till he reached me. This time I wasn't going to be intimidated.

'It's none of your business,' I said.

Gabe didn't seem to take offence.

'Maybe that's true and maybe it isn't,' he said.

I sighed. What did I have to lose? 'I'm leaving,' I

said. 'Can you tell Uncle Jack I'm sorry, but I had to go? In fact, you can tell him it's all Tilda's fault. She's been totally vile to me ever since I arrived.'

Gabe blinked. 'I'll tell him, Matt Crimmond,' he said, 'or the first part at least. But don't you go thinking you can get away just like that. They won't let you.'

I recoiled sharply. 'Who won't let me?' I asked. 'Uncle Jack and Tilda aren't going to stop me. I shouldn't think they care much anyway.'

Gabe's mouth creased up into a sardonic smile and he leant in closer to me. 'Not them, boy,' he said. 'I mean the harbingers. And maybe the gabbleratchet.'

Though Gabe's breath was warm on my face, my body suddenly felt cold all over. Could it be true? Would I really never get away from here? I fought for control. Gabe was talking rubbish, and I wasn't going to listen to it. I stepped back from him, hefted my bag further up my shoulder and started walking as fast as I could. It had no effect. He fell in beside me, wiry as an old whippet.

'Look, just let me go, can't you?' I said.

Gabe stopped dead and pointed. Ahead of us a straggle of round-bellied Dartmoor ponies were cropping the grass at the side of the road. They scattered at our approach. Just two remained, turning in different directions as if they couldn't decide how to make their escape.

And then I saw it, sitting on the road close to the ponies, staring at us. It had to be a hare. Long, long ears tipped with black and huge raised eyes. I'd never seen one before, but I knew what it was at once. Only it didn't move. Just stared at us with those malevolent dark eyes.

Slowly I raised my camera from round my neck. It would run off, surely. But no. It was still there, still staring. I clicked the shutter. That would be some picture.

Gabe jabbed my arm sharply. I put the camera down again, and realised the ponies hadn't found a way out of the road. They were going frantic – twisting and turning, backing away from the hare as if it was the most terrifying thing they'd ever seen. Suddenly one of them reared up on its hind legs, its open mouth flecked with foam. For a moment it towered there, then it brought its hooves down hard against the other one's belly.

There was a high, pained, drawn-out whinny that seared through my brain. Then at last both ponies pounded away.

I looked at the road again. The hare was gone.

Something boiled over inside me. I flung my bag into the road in the direction of where the hare had been sitting.

Gabe watched, expressionless, as I picked it up again. 'You won't get rid of it like that. It feeds on the anger, see. Hares bring evil luck, often enough. I reckon that one there was a harbinger – you saw what it did to those ponies. And there's a good chance that mare would have been in foal. She'll probably miscarry now.'

I didn't want to hear any more. I started walking again.

'You think you can go,' Gabe said, 'but you'll be back.' His voice was softer, almost gentle. 'I'm sorry, boy. There's nothing you nor I can do.'

'What is it with you?' I shouted. 'You can't change my mind, whatever you say. Why don't you go back home to the farm and leave me alone?'

Gabe laughed. 'I was at home already when I saw you coming,' he said. 'It's just over there.'

I glanced ahead and saw a cottage I hadn't noticed before. Not a pretty one, though. The walls were brown rather than white, and in need of a major scrub-up. A ramshackle fence surrounded a small yard full of rusting bits of metal. Four chickens were foraging for scraps among the debris.

'You can come in and have a bite with me and the missus if you like,' said Gabe. 'We're just about to have our tea.' He walked up to the gate of the cottage and waited for me.

'Sorry, I can't,' I said. 'I've got to go.' I squared my shoulders. 'Whether they let me or not.'

'Ah, well,' he said. 'You do what you must do.' He hesitated. 'You'll find there's a bus in Widecombe that takes you off the moor if you hurry. It leaves at ten to four. It's the only one this afternoon, mind.'

'Thanks,' I said.

That seemed to be enough for him. Gabe wasn't like other adults, always fussing about nothing. He just nodded and turned to go through the gate. When I looked back, he was standing at the front door next to an oldish woman with slate-grey hair down to her shoulders. Sort of witchy-looking. Both of them were gazing after me.

I made the bus by the skin of my teeth. There were only about five other passengers, and I sat on my own near the back. For a while I stared into space, then I got out my camera. I wanted to see that hare again. Only when I looked, there was nothing there.

I checked further back. All those pictures from Old Scratch Wood had gone, too. And the ones from the tor on my phone. It was weird. There had to be some kind of fault with both cameras. Unless . . . No. I didn't want to think about it.

Thank goodness I was getting off the moor. Mum would go mad when she found out what I'd done, but right now I didn't care. I took a quick look at my phone. Still no signal. Good. I intended to keep it that way for a while, so I turned the thing off, shoved it in the bottom of my bag and shut my eyes. A plan was forming in my mind. Why should I go home at all? It wasn't like Mum wanted me there. She and Paul the pillock and my pig of a cousin could all stuff themselves. I was going to disappear.

The bus stopped in Totnes. I asked a couple of people for directions, and waited for another bus that would take me on to Dartmouth and the river. I was in luck. I only had to hang around for another hour or so. And finally I was there.

I know the river Dart has its source high up on Dartmoor – Dad had told me that often enough – but by the time it reaches Dartmouth, it's a huge natural harbour with hundreds of fancy yachts tied up all along it. It was a relief to see blue water and shops and people walking around as if they were enjoying themselves – like a burst of sunlight after all the darkness on the moor.

I'd been here a few times with Dad, and I knew where he kept his boat. Not the big yacht he'd set sail to the Canaries with – just a little wooden one he keeps here for pottering about the coast. I bought a pasty and some water and biscuits, then I walked down to the marina and found her. *Dreamcatcher*. She's not much to look at, but two can sleep in her quite comfortably.

I went into the marina office and asked for the keys, giving Dad's name and address. The girl didn't look twice at me, just handed them over.

Success. I was in.

For ages I watched the other boats on the river. I ate my pasty on deck, congratulating myself on my brilliant idea. I even tried to read one of the books Dad had left on the boat – *Knots and Their Uses* – but gave up after I couldn't work out how to do a bowline. Finally I snuggled up in a sleeping bag on a narrow bunk and felt myself drifting off to the gentle rocking of the boat. It was so peaceful. I wondered what was going on at the farm, and hoped Tilda was in serious trouble.

I wished I'd sneaked Jez away with me, just for a bit of company. But never mind, I was fine by myself. Everyone would just have to do without me. Including the gabbleratchet.

12

Kitty

Matt's gone away. He didn't say goodbye. Daddy's very cross with Tilda and she keeps on singing 'It's a lovely day today' so he gets even crosser. But I want Matt to come back. I think the chickens do, too. Our cockerel was horrible to me today. He jumped at me with his spurs and I ran away. He's never done that before – he's always nice. But it wasn't his fault. All the animals are scared. They think something bad's going to happen. And Matt's all on his own.

13

matt

When I woke up to the sound of gulls and clinking masts I couldn't believe I'd stayed out all night by myself. No one had any idea where I was. That would show them – Mum and Paul and Tilda and everyone else. What's more, it had been the best night's sleep I'd had for ages. I stuck my head out of the cabin and inhaled the fresh air. The sun was just coming up, the water was rippling gently and no one was about. I'd got away, despite all Gabe's predictions. What a load of old rubbish they'd turned out to be. And with luck, Tilda would get a major telling-off for her part in my disappearance. She deserved it.

The trouble was, I couldn't help feeling guilty about Mum. She would probably be going spare by now. I hoped she wouldn't start imagining all sorts of terrible stuff had happened to me. I mean, it wasn't like I was a kid any more – I could look after myself. But maybe she'd think I'd gone to a friend's or something. And of course Gabe would have told her I was OK – in fact, knowing him, he'd have said I'd be back on the moor any minute to face the gabbleratchet. Ha ha. Like that was going to happen.

I knew I should call her to let her know I was safe, but I didn't want to yet. *Let her stew for a while*, a dark part of me thought. Maybe she'd think twice about Paul if she started missing me.

I ducked down below again and my eye fell on the box perched at the top of my holdall, containing the curlew skull. Bringing that had been pure genius – it would really annoy Tilda. But I still didn't like it. I stuffed it further down in the bag, under my clothes.

Then an idea occurred to me, swift as a shadow across the water. I was in trouble already, so why not go the whole hog? I could take *Dreamcatcher* out myself. I'd always wanted to sail her single-handed, but Dad wouldn't let me – he said I had to get my Yachtmaster exam first. But I knew how to handle her perfectly well – I'd done masses of dinghy sailing over the years, so it wasn't as if I was a novice or anything. It would be exactly what I needed to get the last few days out of my system – Tilda and the skull and Old Scratch Wood and the way those animals had been acting ever since. But it wasn't just that. Deep down, I realised, I liked the notion of scaring everyone just a bit.

Before I could talk myself out of it, I started getting the boat ready. Dad would go ballistic if he knew, but then he was off floating somewhere on the Atlantic – and besides, he'd left me behind with the four-eyed pillock without a second thought. I wasn't going to worry too much about his feelings right now.

I took a while checking the sails and unrolling a bit of jib, then got the ropes ready. There wasn't much wind down here on the river, and the water was hardly moving. The tide must be just at the turning point, which would make it easy to get out of the berth – I wouldn't have to worry about which way it was going.

Finally I turned the engine on. Even though Dad hadn't used it for over a year now, it purred into action straight away. Great. I put it into gear and slipped the ropes, and *Dreamcatcher* moved slowly out from the pontoon.

'Nice and steady does it,' I said, and laughed, because I sounded just like Dad.

With the slightest movement on the helm, *Dreamcatcher* and I chugged out of our berth and into the river.

I knew the rules of the road, or at least the most obvious ones. I'm good at that sort of stuff. *Keep to the right on the way out. Power gives way to sail. Port gives way to starboard. Windward gives way to leeward.* But I was the only one out. It was too late in the season for holidaymakers, and way too chilly.

I'd only got my jumper and my coat on – totally the wrong kit for sailing, and if it got wet, I'd be cold and miserable. I put the gear lever in neutral and went below to see if there was anything I could find to keep me warm.

I was in luck. Dad had left a couple of thick woolly fleeces rolled up in one of the lockers, and in a cupboard I found waterproofs and a windproof jacket. I stuck on a fleece and felt the warmth seep into me. It was a bad move, though. Suddenly I really wanted Dad here, not just his fleeces. I wished he hadn't disappeared right when I needed him. Mum always said that when the going got tough, Dad got going. I'd always stood up for him – but maybe she wasn't completely wrong. There was no point in dwelling on it, though. I clambered out of the cabin and took the helm again.

A couple of fishing boats covered in huge pink buoys were heading out to the river mouth far ahead, surrounded by hopeful seagulls. I watched them till they disappeared, then chugged after them, taking care to keep to starboard and follow the contours of the river. I didn't think there were any nasty rocks, but it was best not to take any chances. It felt weird being in charge on my own. Dad lets me helm a lot of the time, but he's always there watching me. I wondered if I should maybe go back now. But no – taking the boat didn't really count unless I got out of the river and into the sea.

Dreamcatcher passed the castle, and then the church with its walled graveyard. On the other side, high on the hill, was the stone tower that signalled the entrance to Dartmouth Harbour. I was doing pretty well, I reckoned. Normally Dad and I sail on the Solent, but he'd taken me here a year ago and it was all coming back to me. I turned into the wind and climbed on deck to hoist the mainsail. It was heavy, but it went up smoothly. OK, we weren't sailing properly yet – I was keeping the engine on for a while

– but it felt fantastic to be away from all that craziness on the moor.

Once *Dreamcatcher* and I got out of the river and into the bay, the motion changed. The wind was stronger, and there was a light swell – a gentle rolling up and down that made me smile. I was beginning to feel at home. When I cleared the red buoy, I turned right and headed for the lighthouse at the end of the headland. It's the way Dad has taken me before, and it's a big wide bay with no rocks to worry about, just lovely open sea. I didn't know much about navigation, but figured that wouldn't be a problem so long as I could see the coast. It was time to turn the engine off and do a bit of real sailing.

The first thing you notice is the silence. Then different sounds take over – the slap of the waves, the wind whistling around the sails, the flapping of canvas. I shifted the mainsail round to take the breeze, hauled the jib in tight, and was back in control again. The sails bellied out, taut with the wind. And now we were racing across the waves, free as a bird, and it was the most brilliant feeling in the world. All my worries disappeared into the vast blue-grey of the sea.

The wind was coming from the south-west, so to follow the coast, I had to keep beating into it. That means doing zigzags – the closest you can go to the wind is forty-five degrees, so you have to keep tacking around to keep your course. Only it's quite tiring – you don't gain much ground because you can't go in a straight line.

I wasn't much further on after an hour or so, and I was beginning to get seriously hungry. I wished I'd stocked up on food, but all I had was the biscuits. I shovelled a few down, but they didn't really do the trick – I just felt hungrier. And now sort of lonely, too.

I told myself that I'd go as far as the lighthouse and then turn back. But it was taking ages: the wind was strengthening, and further out to sea I could see a few white caps on the waves. I began to wish I'd stayed in the river – or better still, back in the harbour.

Above the sound of the sea I realised I could hear a high-pitched noise that kept on repeating. My first thought was the sails. I checked them, but they looked OK. The thing is, noises matter at sea. You don't want your boat going wrong. I felt a bit vulnerable all of a sudden.

What's more, the noise was growing louder now – this mournful keening that seemed to spiral higher and higher. I couldn't work out which way it was coming from – only that it was getting closer.

Whistling, I thought suddenly. That's what it was like. A long, melancholy, ghostly whistling, getting louder all the time. My stomach lurched. What if it was curlews? Uncle Jack had said that they were a bad omen for sailors. And here I was, out on the sea on my own. How could I have been so stupid? With rising panic I peered in all directions, searching for the source of the noise, but hoping desperately not to find it.

Then I spotted them. A group of large brown birds, flying low over the water, and heading straight towards the boat. I glimpsed the shape of their bills – slender and curved and very long. Exactly like the skull at the bottom of my bag.

The piercing noise grew louder and shriller. It filled my ears and my head and then the entire sky.

I could make them out more clearly now. They were coming straight for me. *Were* they curlews? I'd no idea if they flew in groups like this. And surely they weren't going to attack? I couldn't believe it. The bills looked like curved swords that could slash through sailcloth – or skin. And I had nothing to defend myself with. I couldn't leave the helm. My fingers gripped the wheel, white to the knuckle. The birds were almost on me and there was nothing I could do.

Then, with just seconds to spare, they swerved upwards – so near that I could feel the rush of their wingbeats on my face. Instinctively I ducked my head and shut my eyes. I sensed more of them flying over me, horribly close. And suddenly I felt a deep raking gash on the top of my head, leaving me so full of pain I nearly fell. I gripped the helm and steadied myself. Then cautiously I opened my eyes and put my hand to my hair. It came back red and wet. But the birds were gone.

I felt dizzy and sweaty, even inside all my layers. They had to be curlews. I couldn't pretend any more. Gabe had been right all along. They were out to get me.

I thought of the curlew skull down below. Did it have something to do with the birds that had just flown over? What if it was calling to them in some weird way that only they could hear? I was trembling. I wanted to run into the cabin, dig the skull out from my bag and throw it into the sea. But I had to stay at the helm. The swell was higher now, and it was taking all my concentration to keep the sails from flapping too hard and maybe even tearing.

Get a grip, I told myself. *Come on, Matt. Just get a grip.*

Another gust and *Dreamcatcher* heeled over towards the waves. My eyes were full of spray, but in the distance I could see dark clouds building. I clung to the helm and wondered what it would feel like to drown.

14

tilda

It's chaos here. Everyone's going completely mental about Matt. He hasn't turned up in London and Aunty Caroline has been phoning us every five minutes for news. Finally she said she was going to drive to Dartmoor this morning with her boyfriend – she would have come straight down last night, only Dad told her she'd be much better off waiting in London to see if Matt showed up at home. Anyway, she totally insisted on coming today.

I don't remember when she last visited. Ages and ages ago, way before Mum died. She never came to the funeral – according to Dad, she couldn't bear to. Just sent that huge posh bunch of flowers and said to call her if there was anything she could do – as if. Still, finally coming here would give her a chance to see how much the farm was worth, I suppose.

I didn't know what all the big fuss was about, personally. I mean, Gabe told us last night that Matt had taken the bus off the moor, so it wasn't like he was lost or anything. Gabe gave us a whole load of guff about his stupid harbingers, too.

'The boy thinks he can be free,' he said, 'but they won't let him go for long. He'll be back soon enough.'

Dad kind of believed Gabe, at least about city boy coming back soon. He didn't think Matt was in real danger, he just reckoned he was really angry – and mainly with me. But even so, Dad was going bonkers over it. We ended up having a policewoman round last night asking all these questions about Matt's state of mind and stuff. You could see that she didn't really think anything had happened to him – she only came because Aunty Caroline was in such a major panic. It was kind of cool, though, a bit like being in some detective story off the telly.

But it was all a big waste of time. I was sure Matt would be absolutely fine – he'd be staying with some posh friends of his and laughing his head off at us. He was just trying to make a point.

But yes, I felt a bit guilty now. So I supposed it had worked.

I thought I'd better smooth things over with Dad, so after I'd got Kitty her breakfast I went outside to speak to him. He was in the cow field on the other side of the farm track, checking on the calves. Though they're five months old, they still want to suckle and they've started really annoying their mothers now. I opened the gate and went over to him, hoping they might have cheered Dad up. Only it turned out he was still really cross, because he gave me this little talk that had me squirming.

'I'm sure Matt'll phone this morning,' he said. 'I'm just praying that Gabe's right and he's hiding out somewhere safe. But you need to do some thinking, young lady. If Matt's back here tonight – and I hope to God he is – you're going to have to be a whole lot nicer to him.'

I tried to object, but Dad wouldn't let me.

'You know perfectly well that the farm business is nothing to do with him,' he said. 'So you can't go on resenting the boy. And listen, Tilda, if you're full of blame, it eats away at you. If you're not careful it can end up ruining your life. And it ruins other people's lives, too.'

I looked away. I wasn't going to apologise. Dad wasn't being fair – he hadn't been exactly friendly to Matt either. Anyway, how could I just pretend that everything was all right? What about the farm and what it had meant to Mum? Was Dad giving up on it – and us? Would he just let Aunty Caroline take it all away? My chest tightened with resentment.

'Tilda's very naughty,' chimed in Kitty, who'd managed to sneak up without being noticed.

'Shut up, dork,' I said. 'What's it got to do with you?'

'Tilda . . .' said Dad, warningly.

'I hope Matt's back soon,' said Kitty. 'He can come and see the geese with me. They're all splashing in the pond. They look really funny.'

'Why don't you jump in and join them, then?' I said.

'Right, that's it, Tilda,' said Dad. 'No more pocket money for you for the next two weeks. And you'd better start having a long hard think about how you've been behaving lately.'

He took Kitty off to see the geese. So it was just me and Jez. I went back to the house with her and helped myself to a huge slice of lemon drizzle cake. Jez sat at my feet in the kitchen and put her paw on my knee, gazing at me with eyes that understood and forgave everything. I stroked her thick black fur, feeling the anger slowly fall away.

Suddenly I had a bad feeling in my stomach. I pushed Jez off and shot upstairs to my room. And guess what? The skull wasn't on my dressing table any more. In all the hoo-hah over Matt, I hadn't noticed. That pig had taken it with him, wherever it was he'd gone. But the skull was mine! It felt like the best thing that had happened to me in a long time.

Matt was going to suffer for this.

15

Matt

My fingers were white around the helm. The water ahead was rippling and darkening, and heavy gusts buffeted the sail, swinging it hard to one side. The main flapped viciously. I managed to get control before the boom swung across, but it was a close thing.

I felt my head again. It had stopped bleeding, but it was really sore. I couldn't believe a bird had done that to me. What was causing it all? I was sure Gabe knew, but he wasn't telling. All he'd done was drop obscure hints. And judging by the weird things I'd seen already, whatever came next was going to be pretty bad.

I really didn't want to think about the gabble-ratchet. That folk tale Uncle Jack had talked about – the pack of creatures rampaging across the moor – had sounded like a far-fetched story. But after those birds going crazy I wasn't so sure.

What I didn't understand was, why me, why Tilda? OK, we hated each other's guts and Gabe had said the gabbleratchet fed on anger, but that didn't explain much. It certainly didn't explain why a flock of curlews would take it into their tiny little skulls to attack me.

The skull, I thought. That had to be it. I'd disliked it the moment I set eyes on it. There was something vicious about it – and somehow it was making things even worse between me and Tilda. We'd been tearing chunks out of each other ever since we'd found it. This time I was going to get shot of it.

I decided to risk leaving the helm for a minute and turned the boat so that it was side-on to the waves. Then I eased myself down through the companion-way into the cabin below and rummaged through my bag. My fingers closed around the box.

It was a bad idea.

The boat bucked violently and a cupboard burst open, spilling stuff all over the floor – tins of beans, cans of drink, plastic bottles. They rolled around at my feet as the boat rocked and shook and creaked. I could smell diesel beneath the boards and felt a whiff of nausea, a sear of acid at the base of my throat. My stomach started turning cartwheels. I had to get out into the fresh air.

Back on deck, I slumped on the wooden seat and drew in salty breaths, trying desperately to calm down. My neck felt hot and clammy. I unzipped the top of my fleece and held it away from my skin. *Focus on the horizon*, I told myself. I tried, but it kept going up and down, up and down.

I could feel my neck getting hotter. Suddenly I scrambled to the side of the boat and heaved over it. And again. I was vaguely aware of patches of vomit clinging to the outside of the hull. Then I just crashed down on the bottom of the deck, praying for it all to pass.

I must have lain there for ages, just wanting to die. I'd never been seasick before – I'd always prided myself on my strong stomach, in fact. Now I was being punished. I didn't care if I went down with the boat – anything was better than this.

It was the rain that jolted me out of it. First a flurry of cool droplets on my face. Then harder, sharper, colder. Rain drummed on the deck and bounced back upwards. Slowly I struggled to my knees and stared out at the dark swell. I had to get back to the harbour.

I fought back the seasickness and somehow managed to turn the boat round to face the way I'd come. Keeping busy seemed to help – it took my mind off the horrible up-and-down motion. But heading towards the harbour mouth was a whole lot choppier than it had been on the way out. The tide must have turned, and now I had the wind behind me and the waves coming towards me, bashing hard against the boat. The rain was pounding down as if a whole ocean's worth was falling on deck. I was getting soaked.

I wished I'd put on the waterproofs before setting out, but it was too late for that now. All I could do was keep my course as best I could. Above me the sky was a sheet of steel. I thought of hot soup and Mum's chicken casserole and sticky toffee pudding with custard. Home had never seemed so appealing.

Helming the boat was taking serious concentration. She was tipping to one side, and I had one foot up on the seat to balance. But every buffet from the waves threw me off and it took all my strength to keep returning her to the course. Some of the waves smashed on the side and spray whooshed up into the boat. My trainers were soaking. My hair was sopping. And most of all, I felt stupid. Stupid for not having prepared properly, and stupid for having thought I could handle her in the first place. This definitely wasn't what I'd bargained for.

I was having to zigzag again to reach the harbour, but I figured it might be faster if I rigged the sails to take the wind directly from behind. Goose wings, it's called. You spread the mainsail out one way and the jib in the other direction, like a goose in flight. I grimaced – geese in flight were the last things I wanted to be thinking of right now. But it was worth a try if it got me into Dartmouth before the weather really kicked up.

Dreamcatcher plunged about a bit while I sorted everything out. But it seemed to work. With the sails spread, suddenly I could take advantage of the wind right behind my back. I could see the tower on the hill that marked the entrance, and made a course for that. We were skimming over the water like a dolphin.

Then it all went haywire.

I'd forgotten that goose wings is the most difficult point of sail. Get it slightly wrong, and the wind whips you round, and you've lost it – which is exactly what happened. One moment *Dreamcatcher* was perfectly balanced between the waves. The next, the boom swung round with a huge crash, taking the mainsail with it.

The boat lunged over and drove hard up into the wind. The jib started flapping madly. And then, with a terrifying rasping noise, it ripped almost in half.

Dreamcatcher bucked and floundered, totally out of control. Everything was clunking and bashing and screeching. Spray soaked me from head to foot. Above the din I was sure I could hear something else – an eerie whistling that made my hair stand on end.

This is it, I thought. *It really is. I'm going to capsize.* The curlews, harbingers, whatever, had done their stuff. The gabbleratchet had won.

I wished I'd phoned Mum when I'd had the chance.

But I had to do something. Anything. I grabbed the mainsheet and dragged the boom in. There was nothing I could do about the jib – it was completely ruined. I wound it in to stop it flogging, then took the helm again. I knew exactly how expensive sails were. If I ever got back, Dad was going to kill me.

I wondered if I should send up a distress flare before it was too late. And I'd need to get down below and radio for help. Channel 16. *Mayday. Mayday. Mayday. This is Dreamcatcher. Dreamcatcher. Dreamcatcher.*

Latitude this, *longitude* that, *immediate assistance required.* Dad had practised it with me so many times I could do it in my sleep. Was I actually going to have to do it for real now?

I looked round at the thrashing ocean. Then, slowly, my fingers tightened round the helm. I had to pull myself together. I had to take charge. And I wasn't going to let the gabbleratchet beat me.

Years of barked sailing instructions began to float back to me. *Get a reef in the sail, you moron,* I told myself. I couldn't believe I hadn't thought of that before. It would cut the wind down and give me loads more control. I should have done it right at the beginning. If I'd had any sense.

I edged to the companionway and found the box of safety clips just inside. Yet another thing I'd forgotten on the way out. If it's at all choppy, you need to clip on to the boat in case you lose your footing. Dad would be horrified if he knew I hadn't done it. I grabbed a clip and fastened one end to the ring on my life jacket, the other to one of the safety wires that runs the length of the deck. Holding gingerly on to the handrail, I inched out towards the mainsail. It wasn't so bad really, even with the rain making straight for my eyes. I held on tight, lowered the sail and put two reefs in, then raised it up again. Now it was about half the size and wouldn't catch nearly so much wind.

I got back to the helm and switched on the engine. It chugged into life. *Dreamcatcher* rocked but stayed upright. I offered up a silent prayer of thanks.

My progress wasn't quick, but it felt a whole lot less precarious. The rain had eased off a bit, though I was sopping wet and my teeth were chattering. But at last I was at the entrance to the river. I steered the boat round the entrance buoy and in.

Almost instantly, the wind died down, and the water was as flat and calm as if nothing had happened.

Now that I was out of danger, other thoughts were sliding into my brain. What would Mum be thinking? I didn't want to imagine it.

My phone. I'd forgotten all about it in the chaos. I slowed the engine to a crawl, dived into the cabin and raced up with it again. I switched it on and miraculously there were a couple of bars. Even out on a boat I was better connected than on Dartmoor.

Loads of messages kept arriving from Mum, but I ignored them. Biting my lip, I dialled her mobile. She answered on the first ring.

'Matt! Oh, thank God!' she said. 'Where on earth are you? I've been worried sick.'

'Listen, Mum,' I said, stopping her mid-flow. 'I'm on the boat, on the River Dart.'

'What!' said Mum. She sounded stunned. 'Are you out on your own? Matt, what on earth—'

'I'm fine,' I said. 'I wasn't, but I am now.'

'Oh, God—'

'Everything's OK. I'm coming in.'

She snapped into sensible mode. 'Be very careful,' she said. 'Are you wearing a life jacket? Good. Call me the moment you're in the marina. We're on our way to your uncle's. We'll talk later. Just make sure you're safe. And I'm calling the harbour master right now.' She rang off.

Not long after, a grey launch came racing up towards me. As I got ready to go port to port, I realised it was the harbour master's. He had a loudspeaker, and he was trying to talk to me. My heart sank.

'Are you all right?' he yelled.

'I'm fine,' I said. 'Everything under control.'

'Your mother asked me to check on you,' he said. 'She sounded very worried.'

The shame of it. I blushed, hoping he couldn't see beneath the wet.

'I'm phoning her now to tell her you're safe,' the harbour master yelled.

'Don't worry, I already have,' I said.

He ignored me. Then he spun round and came up alongside. As I'd been dreading, he read me the riot act. What was I thinking of? Did I know how to handle a boat at all? And just how old was I, anyhow?

I apologised, adding a couple of years to my age, and trying to look as sorry as I could. Finally he gave up.

'Make sure I don't have to do this again, young man,' he said. 'I'm not a nursemaid.' He turned his boat and made off.

I took it very slowly. It was well past midday by the time I reached the marina. I was starving and shattered, and I wasn't looking forward to bringing *Dreamcatcher* into her berth. Getting out had been easy. Coming in again might not be so simple. I put out the ropes and fenders, cut the engine to a crawl and scanned along the line of boats for Dad's berth.

Then I saw them. Tilda and Uncle Jack and Kitty, standing on the pontoon and waving to me. Jez was barking madly. Mum's work again, I supposed. I'd never imagined I'd be so pleased at seeing them again, but I could feel all my muscles relaxing.

'Chuck us your ropes,' shouted Uncle Jack.

I inched *Dreamcatcher* into her berth, and Uncle

Jack and Tilda made the ropes fast on the cleats. I switched the engine off, and found I was shaking.

'We were in Totnes looking for you when your mother called,' said Uncle Jack. 'Gabe told us you'd taken the bus. Here, get that wet stuff off and stick this on.'

He passed me a huge fleece and a heavy green jacket. Tilda held out a towel for me to rub my hair. It was the first time she'd ever done anything remotely nice for me.

'Birdbrain,' she said. But she was half smiling.

I could still feel the motion of the sea, up and down, up and down. It felt great to be warm again. It felt great to be off the water. But a single thought was shrieking inside my head like a power drill: I'd thought I could run away from everything, but I couldn't. I was going to have to go back to the moor. Whatever weird stuff was going on there, I had to get to the bottom of it.

16
Tilda

Matt was a total zombie in the car. He fell asleep about thirty seconds after gulping down a sandwich, so we didn't get a chance to ask him anything. Dad said it was the sea air, but I think he just didn't want to have to explain everything to us. Which wasn't really surprising, given what an idiot he'd been.

Even so, I couldn't help feeling a bit impressed. I mean, Matt had actually nicked his dad's boat and sailed it out to sea – that takes guts. I would never have imagined him doing something like that. It's nice to know that for a posh townie with stupid shoes he's not completely useless.

I hadn't forgotten the skull, though. He'd better have brought it back or there was going to be trouble.

When we got home I had to wait a while to find out, because Dad made me and Kitty do the dusting in honour of the royal visit. Even though Matt had turned up safe and sound, Aunty Caroline was still on her way here.

Finally I escaped and knocked at Matt's bedroom door.

'Come in,' he called. I pushed open the door. He was lying on his bed listening to music on his phone. And meanwhile Kitty and I had been slaving away downstairs – all for his mum.

'So,' I said, 'where is it?'

He knew exactly what I was talking about. He reached down for his bag, rummaged inside it and pulled out the box.

'Here,' he said.

I opened it, took the skull out and held it in my hand. It was cool and dark and heavy. It wasn't exactly how I remembered it – the beak seemed a bit shorter, a bit less pointed – but I still loved it. It was the most brilliant thing I'd ever seen. Suddenly all my dislike for Matt rose again like a bad smell.

'We've got to get rid of it,' he said.

I forced my gaze away from the skull and gaped at him. I wasn't sure if I'd heard him right. But I had.

'I was going to chuck it overboard,' he said, 'only I didn't get a chance because of the weather. So it's up to both of us now.'

A black cloud started gathering somewhere behind my eyes.

'Listen a minute, will you?' Matt said, hurriedly. 'Don't go off on one. It's important.' In a rush he told me all about meeting Gabe, and then about the curlews and how they'd attacked him. 'Gabe said I wouldn't be allowed to leave,' he said. 'And he was right.'

Gabe's nonsense again. I was sick to death of it. I made a move to go.

'No, wait,' said Matt. 'Think about it – all those omens. Old Scratch Wood. The skull of a curlew . . .'

'A *dead* curlew. Dead as a dodo, in fact. And I don't think dodos count among your precious omens.'

'Yes. But a curlew, all the same. The sheep on the way back from Old Scratch Wood. The farm animals yesterday. And when I was leaving, I saw a hare . . .' He stopped and looked straight at me, his brows scrunched together.

'Please, Tilda. We need to do something.'

Alford Library

Customer ID: 63372751227791

Items that you checked out

Title: The skull in the wood
ID: 3114220
Due: 08 February 2022
Messages:

Total items: 1
11/01/2022 10.05

Thank you for using self-service
Why not check out the digital online library?

http://aberdeenshirelibraries.lib.overdrive.com

Suddenly I wasn't quite so sure any more. What if something bad really *was* coming? Then I remembered that the worst thing in the world had already happened to my family. I wasn't going to let myself be freaked out by a bunch of stuff that anyone who knew anything about the countryside would think was perfectly normal.

Matt touched the skull, then jerked his finger away as if he'd been burned. 'We've got to bury it again,' he said. 'Put it back where we found it.'

'You're joking.' There was no way on earth I was going to let him do that.

'I think it's important, Tilda,' he said. 'You don't understand. It's making things worse. It's – I don't know – sort of evil. As if there's something inside it, watching us.'

I scowled. 'You're not having it.'

Matt looked exhausted. 'Then don't blame me if something terrible happens.' He turned over and closed his eyes.

I took the skull back into my bedroom and laid it on my dressing table. The beak was even blacker than before, and it seemed to weigh more now. It wasn't all in my imagination – bird skulls should be super-light, and this one was more like a stone. It was weird. But

I loved it, and Matt could dream on if he thought I was going to let it go.

There was someone who might know more about it. Alba, Gabe's wife. She's really into birds – she knows their calls and everything. She used to teach me about them when I was little and she and Mum were friends, and she tells me where to go on the moor to see interesting stuff. And she's not half-batty like Gabe, though she's into all those stupid stories about the moor, too. If I was quick I could go and see her and still get back before Aunty Caroline arrived.

I packed the skull into its box again, scribbled a note for Dad and told Jez we were off for a walk.

'Don't get too excited, though,' I said. 'It's only round to Alba's.'

But from the way Jez was barking, I don't think she got that bit.

We went across the moor, avoiding the road so I didn't have to put her lead on. The last of the rowan-berries were clinging to the stubby trees along the ridge. Winter was nearly here.

Alba came to the door wearing a purple smock over leggings. She always dresses kind of strange for her age. She's quite tall and thin, and her hair's completely grey but she wears it long. She looks as if she's come straight out of *Harry Potter*. But when she saw it was me and Jez, her whole face lit up.

'Tilda! It's good to see you, lovey. On your own, are you?'

'I just wanted to . . . say thank you for the lemon drizzle cake. It was fantastic. I finished it this morning. And yes.'

'I'm glad you enjoyed it. And Matthew and little Kitty, too, I hope. I'm really glad your cousin's back again. You all must have been so worried.'

I rolled my eyes, but Alba didn't see. She led us through the hall into her sitting room. Everything's kind of brown at Gabe and Alba's. Brownish walls, brown chairs, dark brown wood. Loads of brown-framed pictures all over the walls. I settled into the brown sofa.

'Now you wait there and I'll bring us something nice,' she said.

Jez stretched out at my feet pretending to be asleep, but her nose and ears were alert for the possibility of treats. In a few minutes Alba came through with a Coke and a big slab of millionaire's shortbread for me, and a cup of tea and a smaller bit for her. She sat down opposite me while I laid into it, thanking her between bites. I dropped a sneaky bit down to Jez, too.

'So what is it, then?' she asked. Alba always knows when something's up.

'I've brought a thing I want you to see.'

I took the box out and showed her the skull. She picked it up and stared. Then she put it on the coffee table and looked away.

'It's a curlew,' I said.

'Yes, it is, lovey. I can see that.'

'But it's changing. It wasn't so black before. Why do you think it's doing that?'

'Where did you find it?' Alba asked.

'In Old Scratch Wood. It was buried there.'

Alba's face creased and furrowed, and her grey eyes narrowed. She suddenly looked a whole lot older. She didn't say anything for a moment. Then she took a deep breath.

'It's happening again,' she said. 'Has Gabe spoken to you?' She pushed the skull away.

I knew what she meant immediately.

'All that stuff about strange omens − birds and I don't know what else? Yes. He goes on about them all the time. But it's just stories, isn't it?'

Alba closed her eyes for a second.

'I don't know exactly,' she said. 'Gabe's told me about when everything turned bad the last time. And it was real enough then.'

'What do you mean?' This wasn't what I expected from Alba. The only thing she seems to fret about normally is whether we're eating properly now Mum isn't here to look after us.

'All I know is the birds have come before to Parson's Farm and they'll come again,' she said. 'They're a warning. A warning of evil to come.'

'Not you, too, Alba,' I said. She was freaking me out. Jez whined and pawed me. Alba smoothed her hands over her smock and spoke in a voice so low I could barely hear her.

'Your mother didn't believe it either . . .' She bit her lip and stopped.

'What do you mean?' I said. 'What's Mum got to do with it?'

Alba just shook her head.

'Alba, tell me what's going on!' I pushed Jez away and stood up. The room was feeling much too small for me.

'Your mum didn't believe in anything she couldn't see or touch,' said Alba. She hesitated. 'But you should, Tilda. You should believe in the stories out here on the moor. Birds and animals going bad – people say it's how the gabbleratchet starts.'

'Gabbleratchet.' The word filled my head like the wind on top of a tor.

Alba looked at me and her eyes seemed to bore right through me.

'The gabbleratchet, yes,' she said. Her voice was pale as faded ink. 'You might still have the choice to turn it back. But if not . . .'

This was all getting too much. I wanted her to stop.

'. . . the gabbleratchet will come. And I pray to God you'll never have to see it.' Alba put her hand on my arm. 'Bad blood is what causes it. I know how much you're hurting inside, lovey, with your mother gone. But you have to stop taking it out on other people. You need to learn to forgive – to let it go.'

I moved my arm away. It was so unfair – the one person who I'd thought might stick up for me had turned against me.

'You might be able to stop what's driving it,' Alba was saying, but I was only half listening. My blood was racing in my ears. 'Stop the anger. Pray God you can. I'm sorry, lovey. I really am.'

She got up, gathered the cups and plates in quick, nervous movements and disappeared into the kitchen. Jez whined and pushed at my knee. I grabbed the skull and left.

I stomped down the ridge, rehashing what Alba had said and feeling more and more angry. I should have stood still when I heard Jez bark twice – sharp, urgent barks that sounded a clear warning – but I kept on marching down. And suddenly, unbelievably, there it was in front of me. Something I'd never seen, but always wanted to. A stag with huge antlers, staring at me, sizing me up. Its eyes swivelled in their sockets. I could just make out their colour – one brown, one blue. It lowered its head slightly. Ready to take me on.

I felt my heart clench tight. It was enormous. Its coat was reddish-brown and I could count at least five points on each antler. What was it doing out here in the open? Would it charge me? And what about Jez? She could easily get herself killed.

'Sit, Jez,' I hissed. Jez growled low in her throat, but sat down. Her entire body was tensed to defend me.

I stepped backwards slowly, never taking my gaze off the stag. At last I reached Jez and put my hand on her collar.

'Come on,' I whispered.

Together we inched back some more. The stag watched us, one hoof raised. I could hear its breath coming in short quick pants. I wanted to run – but I knew just how bad an idea that was.

The stag snorted and lowered its head. Its huge antlers aimed straight at us. Every point looked sharp as a blade. All at once I knew it was going to charge.

With a violent bound, Jez broke away from me and hurled herself towards it.

'No!' I screamed. But Jez was right up there, growling and snarling, trying to find a way to get beyond the antlers, trying to scare the thing off.

Suddenly the stag slashed its head towards her. Jez let out this awful whimper and jerked backwards.

Then the stag simply shook itself and turned away. It pounded over the ridge, cleared a hedge and was gone.

17
Matt

Mum had phoned from Exeter to say she was nearly here. She was bringing Paul with her. I knew I was going to get yelled at for taking the boat, and I wasn't looking forward to it.

Gabe had already managed to corner me, too. I'd gone out into the front yard and there he was, getting down from the tractor.

'Back, are you, Matt Crimmond?' he said.

I tried giving him my tough-guy stare. 'Obviously.'

Gabe smiled, but it only reached one side of his mouth. 'I told you, didn't I? But you didn't listen. You can't run away from it. Not by land, nor sea neither.'

Where was he getting all this stuff? I was almost beginning to wonder if *he'd* sent the curlews after me.

'But why?' I asked. 'And why me?'

'Not just you, Matt Crimmond,' said Gabe. 'There's no saying who Old Scratch wants for himself if he sets his messengers gathering. He finds his opportunity . . . he sniffs bad blood like carrion. It's meat and drink to him. And then, if he finds it to his liking, he sends the gabbleratchet. But this farm's had more than its share of ill luck. I know it all from way back.'

I didn't ask how he thought he knew it all – there was no point in getting even more freaked out. Right now I didn't want to hear about it.

'Look, I've got to go, Gabe,' I said. 'My mum's coming soon.'

He nodded.

'I'd best make myself scarce, then,' he said. 'She'll not be wanting to see me. I need to go on home anyway. I've got an idea of something that might keep the evil off.'

Whatever, I thought. There was no time to worry about Gabe. I could hear the car drawing up in the yard – Mum and Paul must be here. I wondered where Tilda was. I was actually quite worried about her meeting Mum, given the way she'd been over the farm

– there might well be fireworks.

But in the end it wasn't Tilda who blew up. It was me.

The first five minutes of Mum's visit were pretty awful. She didn't know whether to shout at me for being so stupid or hug me until I couldn't breathe, and ended up doing both. It was so embarrassing. Kitty was watching with wide eyes, while Uncle Jack pretended not to notice.

Paul was hanging around in the background in a pair of baggy cords and an *I'm-in-the-country-now* cream checked shirt. He's normally in posh business suits but he was obviously trying to blend in – ha ha. He'd had his hair cut really short but it didn't disguise his bald patch, I noticed. But at least he stayed out of it, just told me it was good to see me in one piece and left it at that. I totally ignored him. Finally Kitty broke up the touching scene by dragging everyone into the kitchen for some chocolate cake.

'Me and Tilda made it,' she said. 'It's because Matty's come home. Look what Tilda wrote.'

On the top in chocolate letters were the words 'Welcome Mat'. I wasn't sure whether it was a joke or one of Tilda's digs. But the cake was good. And at least having tea took some of the heat off me.

Mum and Uncle Jack were sort of awkward with each other. Mum was all bright and brittle and talking too much like she does when she's embarrassed. Uncle Jack had gone even more silent than usual. He must still be angry with her about having to sell those fields, I thought.

Paul, of course, was busy pretending nothing was wrong and acting like a right know-it-all. He kept asking Uncle Jack about sheep farming and markets and yields and stuff, even though it was like pulling teeth. Then he turned to Mum.

'So what was it like growing up here?' he said. 'You don't talk about it much, darling.' I cringed as he put an arm around Mum's waist.

'I'm not really the country type,' said Mum. 'Not like Rose was.' She eyed Uncle Jack, then looked away. 'I couldn't wait to escape from all the mud and the rain. Then I discovered London and I never looked back.'

Tilda had sidled in as she was speaking. She looked strangely pale as she stood listening by the door. Then Mum spotted her.

'Tilda, sweetheart,' she said. 'It's wonderful to see you. It's been so long, hasn't it? Goodness, you look grown up. How are you? How's school?'

'OK,' said Tilda. She couldn't have been more frosty if she'd swallowed an avalanche whole.

Mum refused to be put off.

'We were just talking about how I wanted to go to London when I was your age,' she said. 'You must come and visit us and see the sights. I'll take you shopping. How about that?'

'I hate shopping,' said Tilda. Her eyebrows were a dangerous V shape.

Mum laughed. 'That'll change when you get older,' she said. 'Wait till you're sixteen, and then you'll see. You'll be desperate for some bright lights by then.'

'No, I won't,' said Tilda. 'I love the farm. I'm never going to leave it.'

Mum glanced at Uncle Jack. He stepped in quickly.

'Caroline's just trying to be nice,' he said. 'You might want to take her up on it sometime.' He turned to Mum. 'Maybe I've kept the girls a bit too isolated since their mum died.'

'I'd like to go to London,' said Kitty. 'But only if I can bring Jez and the chickies.'

Mum smiled uncertainly. Paul burst out laughing.

Tilda broke in. 'Dad,' she said. 'Jez got hurt. But Gabe's sorted her out. He says she's fine, only—'

'OK, darling,' said Uncle Jack. 'I'll check her in a

minute. But let's just make your aunt welcome first, shall we? She's had a long drive.'

Tilda scowled and looked at the floor.

'How about we take you all out for an early supper?' said Paul, quickly. 'There must be some local pub that does a decent spread. What do you think, young ladies?'

'I'm not allowed to go to pubs,' said Kitty.

'And Dad's made supper already,' said Tilda, snottily.

Served Paul right for being so smarmy.

'It's true, I have,' said Uncle Jack. 'You're welcome to stay, though.' He smiled, but it looked a bit forced. 'In the meantime would you like to see the farm, Caroline? And Gabe's outside somewhere. We could go over and say hello to him. Rose said you and he knew each other way back.'

'Yes, we did,' said Mum, her mouth twisting. It clearly wasn't a good memory. 'To be honest, it's better if you show Paul around without me, Jack. Matt and I will take a little walk up to Far Field. Come on, darling.'

It wasn't a suggestion but an order. I sighed and followed her out. She was wearing shiny black shoes with heels and a smart skirt, but she didn't seem to care about the mud for now.

The reckoning didn't take long in coming.

'What's got into you?' she said as we walked up to the ridge. 'If you were having problems here, why didn't you just ring? You knew we'd come and get you. It was you who was so desperate to go away in the first place. And what on earth possessed you to go out on that boat? How could you? I've been scared to death.'

I looked down. There wasn't much I could say. Mum was only warming up, though.

'You could have smashed the boat up,' she said. 'You could have been killed.'

'It wasn't that bad. But yeah, I know it was dumb. I'm sorry.'

'Surely your father doesn't encourage you to sail on your own?'

'It wasn't his fault. He had nothing to do with it. It was my idea.'

'Well, it was idiotic, Matt. I thought you knew better than that.'

'Yeah, well.' I kicked at a stone. We turned and started walking along the edge of Far Field. The sheep scattered, but neither of us looked at them.

'And can't you at least try to get on with Paul?' Mum said quietly.

I said nothing.

'He thinks you're terrific. He thinks what you did was very brave. Foolhardy, but brave.'

This was truly lame. Like he gave a monkey's about anything I did. Mum registered my silence.

'Matt, I care about him. I care about him very much. Don't you understand that?'

I looked away. She reached for my arm, but I shook her off.

'He's a jerk, Mum. A total jerk. Only you're so stupid that you can't see it.'

She stopped sharply. Across the field a couple of crows screeched, then wheeled off.

'Don't you dare talk to me like that!' Mum's face had gone bright red. 'It's time you started realising the world doesn't revolve entirely round you. You only ever think of yourself, and I'm getting fed up of it. You need to start growing up.'

I was furious now.

'Grow up yourself!' I yelled. 'It's you that's behaving like a stupid teenager with that pillock. And I'm not having him in our house any more.'

'Well, you'll have to get used to it,' said Mum. Her voice was flat. 'Because as soon as I get a divorce from your father, we're going to get married.'

I stared at her, open-mouthed. She moved towards me and I backed away.

'Oh God, I'm sorry, sweetheart,' she said. 'I didn't mean to tell you like that. I've been so upset about you and I've been up all night. I'm not thinking straight. I'm so sorry.'

I could hear her voice shaking, but I didn't care.

'It's this place,' she said. 'Everything always goes wrong here. Rose and I were always fighting. And now you and me.' She looked away. 'You've got to understand that your dad and I are never getting back together again, darling. And Paul is a lovely man. He makes me happy, Matt. You should just give him a chance to get to know you.'

My head was a black swirl of evil-beaked birds, screaming and stabbing. Blindly I pushed away Mum's hand.

'That's never going to happen,' I said. 'Not ever.'

Hot tears filled my eyes and threatened to spill out. Half running, half stumbling, I found my way back along the field and headed for the farmhouse. I raced upstairs to my room and banged the door.

It was probably an hour or so later when Kitty tiptoed in.

'Matty,' she said, softly. 'Are you coming down?

Your mum's going now.'

'Who asked you to stick your nose in?' I said. 'Just get out of my room and leave me alone!'

Kitty's smile disappeared and she backed out fast. I stuck my head under the pillow. When there was another knock, I ignored it. At last I heard the muffled sound of voices in the hall, then the front door opening and closing. Paul's voice boomed out a goodbye. Then the car crunched down the yard.

Good riddance, I thought. *I hope the gabbleratchet gets him.*

18

Tilda

Matt's in a huge strop about something. He's even managed to make Kitty cry, and that's really hard to do. She asked me if Matty didn't like her any more, and I had to tell her of course he did, that he was just upset. Honestly. After all the trouble we went to with the cake and everything.

It must have been something his mum said. She was all tight-lipped and quivery after she came back from their walk, then she whispered something to Paul, and he put his arm round her and got louder and jollier, like he was trying to snap her out of it. Anyway, when she couldn't get Matt to open his bedroom door,

Aunty Caroline decided she'd better go.

'Give the boy some space,' I heard Paul saying to her. 'Don't push him. He'll come round eventually.'

So in the end she and Paul said goodbye and drove off home to London. She can shop till she drops for all I care.

I dished out the casserole Dad had made – a no-show from Matt again – and we ate in near silence. Dad was all quiet because of Aunty Caroline, and I decided not to tell him about the stag. He'd only worry.

I thought of that photo we've got in the hall of Mum and Aunty Caroline when they were both young. Mum's about Kitty's age in it, and Aunty Caroline must be eleven or twelve. She has her arm round Mum, but neither of them looks very happy. Suddenly I sprinted out and picked it up. I was right: Aunty Caroline was wearing a dark velvet dress, and I could just make out the little raised leaf pattern on it. Could it be the same as the scrap of velvet we'd found in the box with the skull? Did the skull have something to do with Mum and Aunty Caroline?

Just what was going on? With Alba acting so strange earlier on, it had begun to feel as if everyone knew except me. I needed to clear my head. I whistled to Jez and we went outside.

It was beginning to get dark – time to put the chickens to bed. In the back yard I persuaded the two that were still up to go inside their shed, then shut them in. All the time, little velvet leaves danced inside my brain. I stopped still and shut my eyes. It was way too much of a coincidence.

Then I heard it. A kind of heavy thud. I glanced around the yard, but couldn't see anything. But there it was again. It was coming from the direction of the tractor shed.

Jez whined softly. I put my hand to the fur on her neck and peered into the doorway of the shed. Straining my ears, I could hear creaking and scrabbling noises that moved up the back wall, followed by a big thump.

Something was on the roof.

My hand pressed down on Jez's fur, willing her not to bark. I could feel her spine tense, but she kept quiet. She really is the cleverest dog in the world. I held on to her tightly, stepped back outside and forced myself to stare upwards. Nothing.

Then I saw it. A dark figure was moving on top of the roof. In one hand it was raising a hammer. In the other hung a limp black shape. For a moment I thought my heart would stop.

All at once I realised what it was.

'Gabe!' I shouted. 'What on earth are you doing up there?'

Jez must have understood. Her spine relaxed and she barked a hello. The figure that was Gabe shuffled over to the front of the shed and peered down. I could just see the top of his ladder sticking up at the back. Evidently that was what the thud had been.

'Is that you, young Tilda?' He held the limp object behind his back.

'What's that you've got there?' I asked. Now that my pulse was slowing I could afford to feel angry. A sigh floated down on the cold evening air. Gabe held up his arm again. From his hand dangled a black bird. It was dead – very dead.

'Shot a crow,' he said. He spread out a wing, splaying its long dark feathers.

I stepped back. 'Yeah, I can see that – just about. And what are you doing with it?' Sometimes Gabe is so weird he almost frightens me. And now was definitely one of those times.

Gabe knelt down so that he could lean over the edge to get closer to me. The crow flopped beside him, one wing outstretched.

'I'm going to be nailing him to the roof. Keep the harbingers off, maybe.'

I shuddered. It was a horrible idea, yet it made a strange kind of sense. A dead crow will keep off other crows. Maybe this one could see off whatever was hounding us.

'Will it work?' I asked. My voice sounded small.

'Can't say. But it's worth a try. Anything's worth a try. You go on in now.'

He lifted his hammer and started banging. I tore my eyes from the roof and took a couple of steps away. Then I remembered the photo. Gabe was around at the farm when Mum and Aunty Caroline were young. He and Alba knew something. And I needed some answers.

'Gabe,' I said. 'What has Aunty Caroline to do with a curlew skull?'

The banging stopped.

Gabe came to the edge of the roof. He stared down at me.

'You know, then,' he said.

I nodded mutely.

'Alba told me you'd got the skull. It's all happening again.'

'What do you mean, Gabe? Tell me. I've had

enough of not knowing.'

He crouched at the top of the roof. For a minute he was silent.

'You get rid of it now,' he said at last. 'It's bad news, believe me. I don't know how you got hold of it, but just you put it back where you found it.'

I stood in the yard and felt a wave of panic surge in my chest.

'No,' I whispered. 'I won't. It's mine. And I love it.'

'You're just like your mother. Reckon this was a waste of time.' Gabe kicked at the pinioned crow, then tramped to the back of the shed and started down the ladder.

In a moment he was standing in front of me, the hammer clenched in his fist.

'Don't fret, young Tilda,' he said, and his voice sounded suddenly gentle, as gentle as my mum's when she used to tuck me up in bed at night. 'We'll just have to wait and see what happens. And hope for the best.'

The moon was up at last, and casting strange shadows.

'I don't know what you mean,' I said. But deep inside, I did. There was no denying it any more. Something bad was coming. Only how could it possibly be any worse than what my family had already been through?

A nasty thought occurred to me, and before I could stop myself, I asked the question that was echoing in my mind. 'Is it you, Gabe? *You're* not the gabble-ratchet, are you?'

His eyes seemed to see straight into my forehead. He gave a short laugh. 'Don't be daft, girl. Gabbleratchet's an old country word, isn't it? *Gabble*, from the noise the geese make. And *ratchet*, well, that's an old word, too. It means hound.'

I believed him. 'Are you sure you can't do anything?' I said.

'Reckon not. There's too much bad.'

'And the gabbleratchet?' I didn't look at him. Even saying the word made me tremble now.

'That I don't know. Best to keep on hoping.'

I shook my head, suddenly angry again. Jez moved closer into me.

'Hope doesn't get us anywhere, does it?' I said. 'It's never got us anywhere.'

'Don't you be saying that,' said Gabe. 'There's always hope. Nothing's happened yet, and maybe it won't. Come on now. Best you go on in directly and get some rest. I'll walk with you to the door. Mind you lock up.'

The three of us trudged slowly up to the house. Gabe waited until Jez and I were inside, then turned and walked back down the yard towards the main gate. I shut the door and bolted it twice. Then I made sure the back door was locked and went round all the rooms downstairs to check that the windows were shut too.

Dad was fast asleep in an armchair with all the farm accounts scattered round him. Jez made straight for the fire, stretched out and closed her eyes. I wanted to wake Dad, but he looked so peaceful I couldn't. Instead I went upstairs. There was no sound from Matt's room and his door was firmly closed. I looked in on Kitty. Dad had put her to bed and she was sound asleep, her red-gold hair a mass of fluff against the pillow.

'Fly away,' she murmured, and I stroked her head. Then I crept out and into my room.

The skull was there waiting for me. I put my pyjamas on and brushed my hair, then picked it up and carried it over to my bedside table. For some reason I wanted it near me.

Bad things might be coming . . . but at least the skull was beautiful. And maybe, just maybe, it had once belonged to my mum.

19

Matt

The geese are flying high over the waves. A string of them, a massive V that forms and reforms as new ones lead the way. The sky is filled with their clamour. My head is filled with the echo of it – whistling, honking, crying, screaming.

The sea changes colour. Now it's green and brown and grey, and the geese fly over tors and fields dotted with tiny sheep. I'm with them, riding the sky, flying at their side. '*Come on,*' I shout. '*Come on.*' There are geese above me, too, wings outstretched and feet tucked beneath, and I'm riding in their slipstream and whistling through the air, pressed so close to them I can feel the warmth of their down. I want to stay with them, join their wild free flight. If this is the gabble-ratchet, I'm sticking around.

But now there are other birds with them – crows and curlews and silent-flying ones I don't recognise that flit like bats on long, pointed wings. And above me the geese are growing, their white breasts darkening and their eyes turning huge and red. They're something else now – I can see black fur and teeth and drool-flecked jaws, and I sense bellies empty as stones and a hunger that drives them. They're hounds of hell, and I can't look at them any more, can't risk a glimpse. They'll tear me to pieces and leave no trace for anyone to find. I'm running before the gabbleratchet, and I know that it's gaining on me.

In and out of the stream of creatures weave others. Crazed hares, leaping by their side. Deer with delicate hooves and bloody antlers, pounding across their path. The grinning skeletons of sheep and pig and cow, with gaping jaws and black holes for their eyes. And I'm running before them all, and I can feel hot breath on my neck, and the hot wet slaver of their tongues lands with burning spatters on my skin.

They're hunting. And I am the prey now. I am the quarry.

Suddenly they're upon me and I'm in the centre of

the pack. Black fur presses against me. And I'm running for my life, running with all the breath in my body, with the darkest creatures of the night behind me in full cry.

I feel the wildness in my limbs. My legs and lungs are filled with the cry of the hunt and the rush of the wind and the dizzy stuttering stars. I take a bugle from my pocket and raise it to my lips and blow, a high-pitched note that trembles and takes flight. And the bugle is a skull, the skull of a curlew, and the sound of the bugle echoes in my brain and fills the night sky.

'*Tally-ho*,' I shout, and I laugh, and the laugh is a baying that rises from my throat.

The wild hunt is running mad, and the trees are rushing up to meet us, small stunted trees that open their arms and usher us in. Inside the wood it's quieter. The creatures mill in a pack, pacing and growling. They lick their lips as I go by. Green fronds brush my hair as I walk into the heart of the trees.

The standing stone draws me in. It is quiet now. But I've seen the gabbleratchet, and now I must pay.

My skin burns. I can almost smell it burning. And more than the entire world I want to go on living. I'll do anything. Anything.

Suddenly I know there's a bargain to be made.

And I know that I'll make it.

I try to think. Nothing.

Then the black oil of my thoughts melds into a shape. Paul has caused all this. It's his fault. If anyone has to die, it should be him. And if he dies, maybe . . . maybe everything will go back to normal with Mum and Dad.

I stammer and shift my feet. Then I stand up straight.

'*Paul*,' I say, and my voice sounds clear and strong. '*I'll give you Paul.*'

Laughter rings out in the heart of Old Scratch Wood.

But the bargain is made, and now they're in flight again, spinning and howling and yelping and slavering. I'm pulled behind them out of the trees and through the air, swept past the wood and into the open sky.

All at once I'm falling. It's a sharp steep drop, as high as a mountain, and I'm hurtling down and down and my life is whirling through the air. Mum's perfume. Dad taking me for my first sail. Paul. A wedding. Fragments. And I'm falling, falling, and the ground is rising to hit me like the marble slab of a morgue. Five seconds. Four. Three. Two . . .

Then I wake, sweating and whimpering on my bed,

and hugging the crochet cover to me for dear, dear life.

First light was creeping through the curtains, weak and grey and furtive, but still light, and I was grateful. The sash windows banged in their frames as the wind tried to force its way in. I couldn't bear to stay in my room a minute longer. There was too much in my head that I didn't want to remember. I got up, threw on yesterday's clothes and headed downstairs.

No one was up yet, and I paced around the kitchen making as much noise as possible in the hope of waking Uncle Jack or Tilda. No one stirred, though. In the end I decided to go and feed the animals. I needed to be doing something, anything, rather than sitting brooding. And at least it would impress Tilda.

It was miserable outside. The wind tugged at me as if it was planning to dismember my body and hide the evidence. I wished I'd stuck on a coat and a woolly hat, and maybe a pair of gloves as well. You'd think I'd have learned that by now, but clearly not. Not this morning, anyway.

I looked in warily at the cow and its calf in East Barn – there was no way I was going to risk a repeat performance of the other day. Right on cue, the huge cow shifted about and stamped her foot. I closed the door fast and left her in the dark.

Even the chickens seemed agitated. When I let them out, they scattered in all directions and wouldn't even come back when I shook out some grain. The cockerel flew straight up on to the henhouse roof and sat gazing at me as if I was his worst enemy, though to be honest I was quite glad he was safely out of the way. Then two dumpy chickens raced off into the distance, flapping their wings madly in a doomed attempt to take off. It should have been funny, but it wasn't. Something was definitely spooking them.

And now I was pretty sure I knew what it was.

20

Tilda

I heard Matt scream in the night – at least, I think it was him. The wind was making a total racket and the house was creaking and shifting, so it was hard to tell what was inside and what was out. I never like it when it does that. And I thought I could hear birds calling, but I probably imagined that bit. I stuck my head under the covers and hoped for the best, and when I woke up again it was morning.

Dad was already up and gone when I came down. I was the only one around. The wind was still whistling and the sky was as grey as the slates on East Barn. All the time my brain was buzzing with worries – the velvet dress in the photo, Alba's face when she saw the skull, Gabe's sudden alarming kindness.

I decided the best thing – even if I didn't really want to – was to talk to Matt about it. To figure out what we should do. But when I tapped on his door and pushed it open, he wasn't there. The bedclothes were all muddled, so he'd definitely slept in his room. Surely he hadn't run away again? But it didn't seem very likely. He must have got up before me – maybe he was actually doing some chores. Wonders would never cease.

I went through to Kitty's room instead. At least she was still in bed. But she wasn't her normal cheery self. Usually I can't stop her bouncing off the walls, but today she was all bleary and didn't want to get up at all. She said her head hurt. I wasn't surprised, with it blowing so hard outside last night. So I told her to have a lie-in and went down again.

Even Jez looked bothered by the wind. She was pacing around, wild-eyed and growling. I opened a tin of food for her and watched her scoff it at top speed.

'Good girl,' I said. 'Come on, let's go and feed the animals.'

It was grim outside. The wind threw itself against me and I put up the hood of my parka to keep it out of my ears. I fed the puppies, but they clearly didn't want to brave the weather, so I left them to snooze on their straw bed. Someone had let the chickens out already and I found them huddled in the tractor barn too. They can cope with a bit of rain but they absolutely hate it when it's windy. I checked in the henhouse for eggs, but nothing yet. They were probably on strike today, and frankly I didn't blame them.

Suddenly Jez started barking. I looked up. There was Matt at the gate to the side yard. I wondered if he'd gone to see the geese – though after yesterday I kind of doubted it.

'Hey,' I yelled. Jez bounded towards him, and I followed. As we got close, Matt jerked and stepped back. He took several paces away from us, his hands out in front of him. It was weird. Jez clearly didn't know what to make of it.

'Get her off,' said Matt. 'Don't let her near me.' He looked straight at Jez. 'Back off,' he said. 'Back off.' His voice trailed away and he muttered something I couldn't quite hear. It sounded like *hell hound*.

Jez stopped and tensed. Her big doggy smile disappeared.

'What do you mean?' I said. I was gobsmacked. So was Jez, to be honest. She flicked her ears and pressed in close to me.

'Look at her eyes,' said Matt in a shaky voice. I looked at him, then down at Jez's eyes. Deep, caramelly, and lovable – just as usual.

'What do you mean, Matt?'

He just stared. He looked terrible, his face white and wild.

'Matt,' I said. 'It's Jez. Calm down. It's lovely Jez.'

For a moment Matt looked ready to run. Then his shoulders dropped.

'I'm sorry,' he said. 'I'm being stupid.' With hesitant steps he walked up to Jez, who whimpered a little until he stroked her head. Her ears went down and slowly we all relaxed.

'Come out of this wind,' I said. 'We'll sit in the tractor barn and then you can tell me what's going on.'

We found a couple of bales and Matt slumped on one with Jez by his side. Lightfoot and Lawless were still curled up, sleeping. Quiet for once. It made a nice change.

'OK, then,' I said. 'I know something happened with your mum. So spill.'

Matt looked away. Then in a bleak voice he explained what had happened – Aunty Caroline wanting to marry Paul. Wow. So that was what had freaked him out. No wonder he'd been so upset. If I was honest, I'd quite liked Paul – he seemed all right, even if he sometimes sounded a bit like those London people who come down here and buy up all the nicest old farms and then don't even farm on them. But I could see it from Matt's point of view too. I mean, no one wants their mum to install a replacement father just like that. I let my mind float for a second over the possibility of Dad marrying someone else. It was too horrible to think about.

'There's more,' I said. 'The skull – your mum knows something about it, and so does Gabe. And he won't say so, but I'm sure he thinks the gabbleratchet's really coming now.'

Matt stared at me, then turned his eyes away. He picked up a wisp of hay and fiddled with it.

'What is it?' I said. 'Didn't you hear me?' I gave a sigh. 'OK, you win. You were right. I'm sorry I didn't believe it before.'

No reaction. I waded on.

'Matt, I went to see Alba. The birds turn into—'

'A hunt,' said Matt. I stared at him. 'A hunt across the skies and across the moor. With all the creatures of hell in full cry. Deer, hares, curlews. Hounds . . .'

'There was a stag yesterday,' I said slowly. 'A stag with funny eyes – one blue, one brown. That's a genetic thing, isn't it? You get dogs like that. Only I thought it was going to attack me. And in the end it went for Jez. It was lucky she wasn't badly hurt.'

'I saw a hare on the road,' said Matt. 'It didn't run away or anything. Just stared. And then these poor ponies it was watching went totally berserk.'

'And there was the cow and the geese,' I said. 'Maybe it wasn't so normal, the way they were behaving . . .'

We looked at each other.

'Dad said if you see the gabbleratchet – the hunt – then someone dies . . .' I said. I trailed off.

Matt wasn't even looking at me. Finally he lifted his head and held my gaze. Although the barn was dark, I took in the fact that his eyes were hazel. I hadn't noticed before.

'I saw it,' he said.

At once Jez stood up and stiffened. I could feel all the hairs on my forearm lift and prickle.

'Where?' I whispered.

'It was a dream. At least, I think it was a dream, it's hard to tell. But I was there, flying with the gabble-ratchet. It was geese first – and then it changed.'

Jez growled low in her throat, and I shushed her. She went over to Matt and stood right up close to him as if to calm him down. He stroked her and smiled. I made Matt tell me it all from the beginning. When it came to the bit about the standing stone and the bargain to be made, I held my breath. Matt faltered and stopped. I waited. Then I couldn't bear it any more.

'Who?' I asked. 'Who did you say you'd give?'

Matt looked at me, and his hands were shaking. He put his arms round Jez and clung to her. Tears glinted in the corners of his eyes.

'I couldn't help it,' he said. 'I had to say someone. So I said Paul.'

Relief flooded through me. Then I realised just how horrible and selfish that was.

'Don't worry,' I said, though my voice wobbled a bit. 'It's not going to happen, Matt. It was only a dream.'

21

Matt

When we got back to the house, Uncle Jack was standing in the hall waiting for us. Immediately I knew something was wrong. A rock formed in the pit of my stomach. I had done it. The gabbleratchet had accepted the bargain. It had happened.

'Paul?' I asked in a whisper.

Uncle Jack looked at me as if he couldn't see me.

'What?'

'Is it Paul?'

'Is what Paul?' said Uncle Jack.

My pulse slowed a fraction. Then a worse thought elbowed its way into my mind.

'Not Mum?' I whispered. All at once I felt shaky and it was hard to stand.

'Sorry?' said Uncle Jack. 'Hang on a minute, Matt.' He turned to Tilda. 'Can you come upstairs with me, darling? Kitty's not well.'

Tilda stared at me. Then she shook herself and shot up the stairs. Uncle Jack followed her. I didn't know what to do, so I followed, too.

Kitty lay under a quilt made of squares of cream and purple flowers, breathing shallowly, her eyes shut. Her red-gold hair had lost its fluffiness and looked damp and dark. Tilda felt her forehead.

'She's very hot,' she said. 'And a bit clammy. Kittykins, can you hear me?'

Kitty thrashed an arm and turned over, knocking the quilt off her upper half. In her pale pink bunny pyjamas she looked tiny.

'I think she's too warm,' said Tilda. She folded the quilt down to the bottom of the bed. Uncle Jack stroked Kitty's arm. Draped over a chair were her skeleton suit and pink tutu. It didn't look as if she'd be dressing up for Hallowe'en tomorrow after all.

'I'm going to call the doctor,' said Uncle Jack. He hurried from the room.

'I can see the birdies,' Kitty murmured.

Tilda flinched. She leant over Kitty's bed, but Kitty didn't say anything else. Then she turned to me. Her gaze was hard and vicious.

'You offered Paul,' she said in a fierce whisper. 'But I think it wants Kitty.'

My mouth dried. It wasn't true. Not Kitty. She'd done nothing to deserve it. It *couldn't* be true. But then I remembered the terror of my dream and how I thought I was going to be torn to pieces. I knew I'd have given anything to go on living just one more minute. And the gabbleratchet knew it, too. Suddenly Kitty's illness made a dreadful sort of sense.

I couldn't bear to look at Tilda. Instead I stumbled out and down the stairs. In the living room I could hear Uncle Jack on the phone asking for a doctor. He sounded angry, though maybe it was just that he was afraid. I went into the kitchen and sat down at the table. I was responsible for all this.

Jez must have understood how bad I was feeling. She trotted up to me and put her paw on my knee. I threw my arms round her neck and buried my face in her fur. She stayed for a minute or two, then whined softly and wriggled away. I could hear her patter up the stairs and Tilda's voice saying, 'Good dog, good dog.' Jez to the rescue. Not a devil dog at all. What an idiot I am.

Uncle Jack's face appeared at the kitchen door.

'The doctor's going to come if Kitty's still got a temperature this afternoon,' he said. Worry lines were lasered into his forehead. Then he seemed to remember he was talking to me. 'Oh, and Matt, your mum rang. Call her back, won't you?'

I rang the house from the landline in the hall. Paul answered, and for once in my life I was actually pleased to hear him.

'Very good of you to call, Matt,' he said. 'Very good indeed. Bit of a shock for you, yesterday, eh? Anyone would be knocked for six. Please don't panic, though. Nothing's going to happen straight away. I just want to make your mum happy. But you'll be wanting to speak to her, not me rabbiting on like this.'

He put Mum on the line. For five minutes I listened to her apologising and cajoling and reassuring. It washed over me entirely. All was well back in London. It wasn't them the gabbleratchet wanted. It was poor, lovely little Kitty, who wouldn't hurt a fly.

By the afternoon Kitty didn't seem any better. Worse, if anything. I went into her room for a bit, braving the wrath of Tilda who was perched on the side of the bed, and she looked hot and feverish and restless. She was mumbling something in her sleep. I leant over her bed to listen. It was hard to distinguish, but I was sure that I heard the word 'gabble'. I shivered and slipped out.

The doctor – Dr Henderson – finally got here at half past three. She took off a huge puffa jacket and shook out her hair in the hall.

'It's dreadful out there,' she told me and Tilda cheerfully. 'Blowing a hoolie.'

She had a quick word with Uncle Jack, then went upstairs with him and disappeared into Kitty's room. I sat at the kitchen table again and stared into space, while Tilda did a good imitation of a caged tiger. We waited in silence for ten minutes or so. Tilda's prowling got faster. Then Uncle Jack appeared with Dr Henderson.

'We're not sure what it is yet,' she said in a bright voice, as if nothing was the matter. 'It might just be a virus. It could even be the flu. Her glands are quite swollen, but it's the high temperature that concerns me. We'll monitor it, and if she gets more feverish, we'll have to do something quite fast. So I want you all to watch her carefully.'

Tilda and I exchanged glances. I almost said something, but stopped myself just in time. To mention the gabbleratchet would be ludicrous. Especially in front of a doctor – I'd sound like a complete idiot. And it would only upset Uncle Jack.

Dr Henderson said her goodbyes, put on her jacket and headed off. Immediately Tilda raced up to Kitty again. I knew she didn't want me there, but I trudged up the stairs after her anyway.

Kitty was no different. She seemed fast asleep. Tilda hovered over her anxiously, but there's only so much smoothing of covers anyone can do. She had to face me. Finally she looked straight at me. Her eyes were like stones.

I jumped in first.

'Look, I'm sorry,' I said, rushing my words out before she could say anything. 'I didn't mean this to happen. But you mustn't worry, the doctor will look after her.'

Tilda laughed. But it wasn't a good sound.

'The doctor doesn't know what's wrong,' she said. 'And we both know why that is.'

Her body was a wall of hate. Then all of a sudden it lost its hardness. I could see tears well in her eyes, waiting to fall.

'Oh, Matt,' she said. 'I know it's not your fault

really. It's everything. You fighting with your mum. The way the farm's going to be split up. You and me at each other's throats. And something wrong between my mum and yours. Bad blood, Gabe calls it. It's all bad blood.'

She dropped her voice to a whisper.

'And Kitty might die because of it.'

22

kitty

It's really really hot. My head's hot. Too hot. Come here, pretty birdies. Come and sit with me. Come and sing to me. Fly with me.

23

Tilda

It's terrible. Kitty's been taken to hospital. The ambulance has just gone now, and Dad's gone with her. Her hair was all damp and stuck to her head, and she looked so little. I wasn't allowed to go too.

Dr Henderson arrived first thing this morning. Dad said Kits had been getting worse in the night, and by this morning she was talking nonsense and her skin was hot and clammy. Dad was trying to sound calm but I knew he was panicking underneath. And when Dr Henderson made a call, the paramedics arrived really quickly and put her on a stretcher and took her away.

But she wasn't going to get better, even in hospital. Dr Henderson didn't know that, but I did. Unless I could stop it, Kitty was going to die, just like Mum did three years ago, and I'd never ever see her again.

I couldn't let it happen. I couldn't. Dad had told me I was to wait here for Alba to come over when her shift at the café had finished, but I wasn't going to. I knew what I had to do now. Matt was right. Gabe was right. Nothing was going to change until I took the skull back to Old Scratch Wood and buried it again. Ever since we found it, the bad things had kept on coming.

Matt wasn't awake yet. He must have been down in the night, because the biscuit box was out in the kitchen and he'd left a load of crumbs all over the worktop. I could understand why he hadn't been sleeping – I was amazed I'd managed to, with Kitty being so ill. But this morning he was out for the count all through everything – Kitty hallucinating, the doctor arriving, the ambulance taking her away.

So it was down to me. I was going to have to go back to Old Scratch Wood. I thought of the last time and all the noises in the clearing when we found the skull, then realised it was better not to think about it at all.

In my bedroom the skull was waiting for me. I tucked the scrap of velvet carefully around it. Yes: the leaf pattern was exactly the same as the one in the photo of Mum and Aunty Caroline that now stood on my dressing table. I wondered what had happened between them to make them so angry with each other. And just what was their connection to the skull?

I laid it in its box like a jewel. There was no way I would let it get broken, even though I was going to have to part with it. It was such an extraordinary, precious thing. I didn't want to let it go. But there was no other way.

Jez wasn't around, worse luck – Gabe had borrowed her for something to do with the sheep. I didn't want to go without her, but I didn't have a choice. I let the chickens and geese out and fed the puppies quickly. I wondered whether to take them with me instead, but they were just too boisterous, and I didn't want to lose them on the moor.

'Sorry,' I told them. Lawless stood up on his hind legs, almost knocking me over, and I knew it was the right decision. 'You can have a run later, I promise,' I said. 'But right now it had better just be me.'

Finally I left a note for Matt, explaining about the hospital and Alba coming, and saying I'd gone out for a walk. Then I set off towards Thieves' Tor. If I was quick, I could get to Old Scratch Wood in an hour. I'd be back again by mid-morning.

The sky was grey again and it was drizzling just enough to be annoyingly damp and gloomy. I knew this bit of the moor really well, but to be safe I was keeping to the proper bridle path. Beside the path, the bracken was dank and brown and slimy. It didn't look as if anything would ever come alive again.

Up on Thieves' Tor it was even wetter. A herd of Dartmoor ponies stood among the giant stone stacks, cropping the grass and trotting off when I got close. I ignored them and started straight off down the path on the other side of the tor.

I couldn't stop thinking about my sister lying weak and helpless in a hospital bed. She's never like that. Never. Healthy as a prize lamb, Dad always says. Some of my friends don't get on with their brothers and sisters, but I've always loved Kitty. She's just so – well – sunny. It sounds corny, but she's truly sweet and cheerful and likes everybody.

She *couldn't* die. She couldn't follow Mum and disappear from my life. I wouldn't let her.

I tried not to let my mind run away with me, but I kept seeing her with tubes hooked up to her and the doctors shaking their heads. That's what happened to Mum when she was run over. When Dad and I got to the hospital we weren't even allowed to see her. And then she was dead.

At the dry stone wall I quickened my pace. The drizzle was harder now. Normally I love being out on the moor on my own – but then normally I have Jez with me. And today it was so grey and horrible, and the rain meant I couldn't see that far ahead. It doesn't take much to make the ground wet here, and it was getting fairly muddy in parts. But it wasn't really the weather that was worrying me. And though I was totally freaked out about Kitty, it wasn't that either. It was something else, though I couldn't pinpoint it exactly. My ears seemed to have become super-sensitive, picking up all sorts of tiny sounds around me – splashes and squelches and thuds made by I don't know what. The wind and the rain, I told myself. Only maybe it wasn't.

I came across a couple of sheep tucked into a hollow, and they took fright and ran away. No other people, though. In fact, I hadn't seen a single walker since I set off. Lightweights, all of them, I thought. Come summer and they'd be up and down Haytor like yo-yos, as if there was nothing else to see on the moor.

But right now, I wished there were a few of them around, so I had some company. And to keep my mind from conjuring up the gabbleratchet.

My hand went to my rucksack where I'd stashed the box containing the skull. *Stay focused on that*, I told myself. *Give it back, and maybe, just maybe, Kitty will be spared.* We should never have taken it away in the first place. I'd been crazy to hold on to it. Keeping it on the farm was wrong. Too much bad had happened there already. The skull belonged to the moor, to Old Scratch Wood, maybe even the devil himself. And now he wanted it back.

I tried hard not to look back over my shoulder every two minutes – it was only making me more jumpy. The dry stone wall I was following was coming to an end, joining another longer wall that leads out towards the valley – the route I had to follow for Old Scratch Wood. There were a couple of bare and weather-beaten rowan trees in a sad little cluster near the corner. As I drew close to them, I turned to follow the new footpath through the dead bracken, with the wall to my left.

The drizzle was becoming a solid sheet of freezing moisture that clung to my hair and eyelashes. It wasn't the kind of weather you want to be walking in, especially on your own. Even if you're on a mission. A mission for Kitty.

Stop whingeing, I told myself fiercely. *Another half an hour and you'll be there. Half an hour of getting wet. Big deal, girl. Just get on with it. For Kitty's sake.*

And then the fog came down.

At first I couldn't believe it. Everything had turned grey. Grey and damp and eerily quiet. Suddenly I was aware of the scrunch of my boots. There was no birdsong. Only my boots and the wet bracken beneath them and rush of my blood in my ears.

For a minute or two I kept on going, but I could feel the fear building in my chest. I was alone on the moor. I hadn't told anyone where I was heading. And like a complete idiot, I hadn't taken notice of the signs in the weather.

'Fog can be a killer on the moor,' Mum had always said. 'It can come down so suddenly you lose all your bearings. You've got to promise to take care.'

She'd said it so often I could remember her exact intonation. Suddenly it brought her back to me so clearly I could almost touch her. Only she wasn't there. I couldn't see more than a few metres ahead – beyond was a wall of grey silence. I had no idea what might loom out of it into my path.

I scrabbled around in my pocket, which was full of the kind of stuff I always carried just in case it might turn out useful some day – string, a box of matches, a penknife, my compass. At the bottom I found what I was looking for: a bar of chocolate. I unwrapped it and broke off a large chunk, eight or nine squares, and crammed it into my mouth. The warm sweetness melted over my tongue and for a few minutes I felt almost cheerful. Then it was gone. I would save the rest – I might be needing it.

My boots squelched in mud. It was getting soggy underfoot and I realised I must be swerving off the path. I made to the left – at least I knew the wall was there. Only it was getting muddier. The ground was changing. There were clumps of reeds, brown and hollow, but nonetheless spelling out in large letters what I was trying to ignore – danger. I was walking into boggy ground.

I veered further to the left. I must be more off the path than I'd thought. Tufts of reeds were sticking out of puddles. I didn't know how deep the puddles were, so I was having to step from tuft to tuft to avoid them. Some of the clumps of green I was choosing were deceptive and my foot sank down before I quickly replaced it on something more solid. Could I have lost the path so much that I was facing the other way, with the wall to my right? It seemed incredible, but I knew deep down it might be possible. The fog was totally disorientating. It felt like I was in a tiny padded cell that moved with me at every step, its walls just out of reach. I clamped down the rising panic in my throat and tried veering right instead.

Only it didn't get any better. My boots were already clagged with mud, and it was tough work finding a solid spot to stand on every time I took a step. I tested each clump gingerly before I put my full weight on it. If it gave, I pulled my foot back fast. I was beginning to wonder if it made more sense just to splash through the puddles, but at the back of my mind I was thinking *mire*, and splashing didn't seem like such a great idea. On Dartmoor, the valley mires are deeper than ordinary bogs – people can sink up to their necks in them and drown. I didn't think I was anywhere near one right now. But I couldn't be sure.

If only I had Jez with me. She was my protection – Gabe had always said so. She would find her way out of here in a minute. But there was no point in thinking like that. I was on my own now.

Beyond me, something shifted a fraction. I froze mid-step, balancing on a tuft of bog grass. I was being watched. Though I couldn't see anything, I could feel it there, eyeing me up through the wall of fog. What was it? It felt big. Maybe it was out hunting. And caught in a bog in the middle of nowhere, I was the perfect prey. My whole body stiffened. Fight or flight? My frozen brain refused to give the order for either.

I don't know how long I stood there. Whatever it was must be watching me, deciding. I couldn't afford to take so much as a breath. Then, somewhere in front of me, I heard the suck of mud and my heart lurched. It was on the move – and I was directly in its path.

Then it broke forward, splashing and stamping. A rush of black and it was gone. My lungs filled with air again and I stood on my pathetic little tussock, trembling with shock. I didn't know what it was for sure. Not a sheep, though it might have been about the size of one. Could it have been a pony, or maybe even a goat? I'd not seen them run wild on the moor before, though maybe some farmer had started keeping them. Yes, a goat, I told myself. That must be it. Nothing to worry about at all.

I wished I could turn my brain off, because it whispered something to me that I truly didn't want to hear. *Goat's horns. Goat's hooves. The signs of the devil.*

I considered my options for a moment. Suddenly I

remembered my compass. I couldn't believe I hadn't thought of it before. I took it out with shaky hands and consulted it. Old Scratch Wood was north-west of our farm. That was the way I would go. Then I stepped forward into the brown waters of the bog.

24

Matt

When I found Tilda's note I freaked out. While I'd been sound asleep in the early hours of this morning, making up for all the time I'd stayed awake worrying through the night, Kitty had been taken off to hospital in an ambulance. It was like a punch in the guts. I'd never see her again. I knew, with a horrible certainty, that she wasn't going to recover – the best doctors in the world wouldn't be able to stop the gabbleratchet from claiming her. And it was all because of me.

The house was empty. There was no sign of Jez, and Alba wasn't here yet. I walked from room to room. The only sound I could hear was my breath, jagged and unnaturally loud in the silence.

Then it struck me. Tilda wouldn't just be popping out on some jaunt when her little sister was so sick. It had to be something more important. I charged up to her room and started searching frantically. My hunch was right – the skull had gone.

If Tilda had taken it with her, that meant she was intending to bury it herself in Old Scratch Wood – it was exactly the sort of mad thing she would do. Only unlike me, she hadn't witnessed the gabbleratchet. Dream or no dream, I'd seen it, and I knew how it filled your ears, demanding its prize, not taking no for an answer. It wanted a corpse. For all I knew, it might pick on Tilda, too.

I looked out of the window at the sky. I didn't know much about the weather round here, but even I could see that it was getting foggier and foggier. If Tilda didn't get back soon, she might end up the same way as Kitty. Suddenly none of the fighting and the nastiness of the last few days seemed to matter any more. I might not be able to do anything for Kitty, but at least I could try with Tilda. I had to find her.

I threw my clothes on and went in search of Gabe. If anyone understood what was going on, it was him. And right now I needed his help.

I came across him in Long Field, which was now full of sheep, forking hay into feeders in the dense grey drizzle, his hat wreathed in a mist of water drops. Jez was there, too, which wasn't good – I'd been hoping she was with Tilda, keeping her safe, helping her find her way home in this weather. Gabe stopped what he was doing and put his pitchfork down.

'How's the little maid?' he said. 'You heard anything yet?'

'Not yet,' I said. 'Uncle Jack hasn't called from the hospital.'

The light went out of his eyes. Everyone adores Kitty, even grumpy old misery-guts like him.

'Listen, Gabe,' I said, 'you've got to help me. Tilda's not here. She's out on the moor.'

Gabe's mouth tightened. For a moment his expression was unreadable. Then he grabbed my arm.

'Come on, then, Matt Crimmond,' he said. 'What are you waiting for?' He called to Jez. Then, before I knew it, he'd steered me out of the field, shut the gate and we were on the farm track.

A woman with long grey hair was hurrying towards us. I realised I'd seen her before – Gabe's wife, with the witchy-looking clothes. She rushed up to Gabe.

'I got Linda to cover for me in the café when I

heard,' she said. 'I was just about to go over to the farm.' She nodded to me. 'To give you and Tilda a hand, my dear. Good to meet you at last, Matthew. I'm Alba Tucker. It's a dreadful thing about Kitty. You must all be so worried.'

'There's more,' said Gabe. 'Young Tilda's gone off. She needs to be found before something happens. Fog's closing in.'

Alba inhaled sharply. She turned to me, wiping her hands on her skirt and tucking a stray wisp of hair behind her ear. It was hard to tell what age she was. Her oval face was unlined and it sort of drew you in and kept you there. She gave me a brief smile.

'You did right to come to Gabe,' she said. 'I'll run ahead to the cottage and get a hot drink ready for when you find her.'

If, I thought. But I kept my doubts to myself.

'Meet me there in a few minutes,' she said. She legged it back up the farm track and disappeared.

All I wanted was to find Tilda. I tried to tell Gabe we had to go straight away, but he stopped me with a hard look.

'You have to respect the moor, boy,' he said, curtly. 'She'll be throwing everything she's got at that cousin of yours. So you need to be prepared.'

I knew when I was beaten.

It was odd walking with Gabe again. I was only too aware of the last time we'd done it, when I was desperate to get the hell out of here. This time was different. There was a sense of purpose to it – and I felt Gabe was on my side.

We turned right at the end of the farm track and on to the road. As we rounded the bend, there was his cottage. Gabe pushed open the gate and Jez trotted through ahead of him. Impatiently I followed them.

Alba appeared at the door with an old rucksack. 'There's a torch, a compass and a blanket in there,' she said. 'And some food and a flask of tea.'

I took it and thanked her. 'Let's go, then,' I said to Gabe.

He scratched his chin. 'I'll put you on the right way,' he said. 'But I can't help you with this. You're going to need to do it on your own. You set it off. Only you can fight it.' He glanced at Alba, who gave the slightest of nods.

My heart lurched. I'd always thought Gabe was crazy, and here he was, sending me out on the moor on my own in thickening fog. Mum would have a heart attack if she knew. But maybe he was right. Kitty was in hospital because in that awful dream I'd only cared about saving my own skin. Perhaps I could make up for it now.

'She'll have gone to Old Scratch Wood,' I said. 'I think she's taking the skull back there.'

Gabe and Alba exchanged a look I couldn't decipher.

'That's bad,' said Gabe. 'There's more evil in that wood than the girl can handle. Let's hope she didn't get there before the fog came down. You should be able to reach her still.'

'I'm not sure if I can remember the way,' I said nervously.

'Jez'll show you,' said Gabe. 'She'll lead you to her. I'll come with you as far as Thieves' Tor. But then it's up to you.'

Alba touched his arm. 'You'd better tell the boy,' she said. For the first time I noticed how beautiful her voice was – low and musical and compelling.

'Tell me what?' I said.

Gabe looked at the ground. 'All right,' he said finally. 'But we'd better get off.'

I turned towards the road. The fog had arrived in earnest, and I couldn't see as far as the fence. The bits of old machinery that graced their yard had disappeared in a world of grey.

'And you, Matt,' said Alba, 'make sure you leave the anger behind. Bad blood is what it feeds on. It's time to let it go.'

I stared at her, confused. Gabe said nothing. Suddenly I felt ashamed. I'd been so bound up in my own misery that no one else had mattered. I'd upset my mum really badly. I'd never given a thought to Tilda losing her own mum. And now my selfishness might have killed Kitty.

There had to be a way to change things. I wanted more than anything to make them right again.

Gabe put a lead on Jez and handed me a stick from beside the door.

'Good luck, now,' said Alba. 'I'll pray for you and for the little girl.'

We turned back down the road till we'd almost reached the farm track again. Then Gabe cut off up a bridle path on the other side. I was pretty sure it was the way I'd gone with Tilda before, but the fog was so thick now I couldn't see any of the landmarks. We trudged in silence up to Thieves' Tor, Jez running between us.

From the top of the tor the fog looked even worse. How was I going to find my way in this? I hoped Jez knew her stuff. Without her I really would be lost.

Gabe stopped and faced me. 'Perhaps Alba's right,' he said. His voice rang out in the swirling mist. 'You need to know this. Because it's your mother and Tilda's who set everything off the last time the animals went bad.'

For a minute I couldn't speak. Gabe must have seen my face, but he carried on.

'You see, Rose and Caroline were always fighting,' he said. 'Young Rose was the apple of your grandmother's eye when she was little. Your grandmother spoilt her rotten, and Caroline got left out, didn't she? I was older, but I knew Caroline back then, and it was hard for her. She always thought she was second best.'

Now I wanted to hear everything. 'I knew they didn't get on,' I said. 'I just didn't know why. No wonder Mum wanted to get away. So what happened?'

'I'm coming to that, boy. It all started when Rose found an injured bird on the moor. A curlew.'

I held my breath.

'Caroline said she should just leave it, but young Rose insisted on taking it home and trying to care for it. I told her it wasn't the kind of bird you keep on a farm, and would bring bad luck, but she wasn't having any of it. And of course it didn't thrive – a wild thing like that, cooped up in a box. In the end, Caroline asked me to put it out of its misery. So I did what I would for a magpie or a crow, didn't I? I wrung its neck.'

I winced. The fog pressed in on me and its cold crept down my spine.

'Only young Rose went mad when she found out,' Gabe continued. 'She kept its body till the maggots came, and in the end she had nothing but a skull. She loved that skull – she kept it with her all the time, like it was a toy. And she changed. From being just a bossy, spoilt little thing, she turned proper evil. I wondered then if something more than just mischief had got into her. It was like she was possessed.'

The photograph pressed in on my brain, Mum with her arm round Rose, looking desperately unhappy.

'That was when the birds started turning, and the animals after. Till your mum decided to do something about it.'

'Mum took the skull, didn't she?' I said.

'Exactly. Caroline was that worried. Somehow she got the thing away from Rose. And she asked me to go with her to Old Scratch Wood to get rid of it.'

'But why?' I said. 'Why there?'

'Everyone round here knows that the devil kennels his beasts in Old Scratch Wood. And curlews are ill-omened birds. They're dark creatures, his creatures. It felt right to take a thing that was causing so much bad to the heart of evil there. It wouldn't be the first time.'

Suddenly my head filled with the crazed creatures of my dream and I could hear the high shrill note that spurred them on, faster and faster. Now I remembered. It had come from the devil's hunting horn – the hollow skull of a curlew.

'We buried it there,' Gabe went on, 'and we were proper scared, though we didn't see anything to hurt us. I said the Lord's Prayer all the way through, mind. But after that, we reckoned we'd broken the spell of it. Young Rose blamed your mother for the skull being gone, but she didn't know where to look for it. And gradually she came back to normal – though I don't think she was ever good friends with Caroline afterwards.'

'So nothing happened?' I said. Maybe it was all an old wives' tale after all.

'Nothing – until about three years ago. My Alba was friendly with Rose, see. And she told me about a fight Rose had on the phone with your mother. A big one, it was.'

The fields. That would have been what that was all about. Aunty Rose would have been furious about giving Mum the money for the fields they'd had to sell.

'Caroline must have told Rose where we'd buried the skull. Maybe the two of them got back to squabbling over all those childhood things and Caroline just gave in. Maybe she told her in anger. But whatever it was, Rose went to look for it the next day, though Alba begged her not to. She went to Old Scratch Wood. Only she didn't come back, did she? She was run over on the moor, near the wood. They never found the car that did it. She died that very night.'

I stared at Gabe, speechless. How come Mum had never said anything about this? Was it all her fault, or just a really nasty coincidence? No wonder Mum hadn't wanted to go to Aunty Rose's funeral. She must have felt so desperately guilty.

'What do you think it was?' I said. It came out as a whisper.

'I reckon she saw the gabbleratchet – then paid the price.'

And now my cousin was out on the moor with the skull that had caused so much evil and no one to help her.

'We're wasting time,' I said. 'I've got to find Tilda.'

Gabe patted Jez, then looked at me and nodded. 'You'll do,' he said.

He strode away, and Jez and I turned to face the moor.

It was like being drowned. The fog was in my eyes and up my nose and filling my lungs. Whenever I breathed in I inhaled millions of tiny droplets. I hated it.

'Find Tilda,' I told Jez. 'Find Tilda, there's a good girl.'

Jez surged forward, pulling on my arm, and I stumbled behind her through the grey pall. Every so often I stopped to shout Tilda's name a few times. It felt totally weird yelling out into the mist and the sound being sucked into nowhere.

I thought of Mum and Aunty Rose, and how sad it all was. And then I thought of Kitty. If it had ended like that for Aunty Rose, what hope did I have of changing anything? What could I do to stop the gabbleratchet? For the first time I could remember, I started to pray.

The next hour or so passed in a sort of dream. Jez led the way, her nose down to the ground, and I followed. Around us flowed the deadening white fog. I felt like I was walking on the moon. I called and called, and the sound dispersed in the dense air. Nothing replied. I hoped Tilda hadn't made it into the wood.

At some point we turned a sharp right, and the footpath grew bumpier and muddier and harder to track. But we kept on going at the same pace, trudging on, calling and calling again.

And all the time, flickering on the back of my brain, the wild, crazed creatures of my dream. Out on the moor. Hunting.

25

Kitty

Hot. So hot. Red tongues. Red eyes. Red. I can see them all up in the sky. Nice birdies. Nice doggies. Come down, all of you. Come to Kitty.

Gabble. Gabble. Gabble.

26

Tilda

I followed the tiny needle on my compass, past caring about the bog. My boots were thick with mud. It was spattered all the way up my jeans, too, but it didn't matter now. I splashed and squelched through it like it wasn't there. It wasn't going to suck me down. No way. I'd messed up, big-time, but I wasn't going to end up like some pathetic tourist who didn't understand the moor. Kitty needed me.

I floundered through the reeds, grabbing tufts of them to steady myself. Once I fell, and my hands got as black and filthy as my legs. The grey fog moved with me. It was out to get me – mean, creepy, lung-invading. It wanted to take me over, to fill my mouth and my nose, choke me. It wanted to break me. I wouldn't give it the satisfaction.

When I first felt the ground harden beneath my feet I thought that I was imagining it. It was true, though. Slowly the reeds disappeared, the livid green turning to damp brown. And at last there was dead bracken and a fiercely blooming gorse bush, a brilliant flash of yellow in the blanket of grey. I felt so grateful for that yellow. It made me feel safe, for now.

Soon I came across a track that might well be the path I'd gone off in the first place. I took a chance and crossed it, and in a few minutes I was at the wall, the lovely, solid, comforting dry stone wall. I crouched there like a sheep trying to get out of the rain.

The trouble was, I was getting colder and colder. People die of hypothermia on the moor, way more often than you'd think. You don't realise it at first, but you start having weird thoughts, then you can't talk properly, and soon you're babbling like a maniac and unless they get to you fast and warm you up, you're a goner. I hoped it wasn't happening to me.

But Kits was the one who mattered here. For her sake, I knew I had to get rid of the skull. I didn't want to do it here, though – it was all wrong. This wall had been put up by generations of farmers, decent people who had nothing to do with the wild hunt or anything remotely spooky. It felt safe and friendly and good.

And I couldn't just go and drop the box in some dank old watery hole back out in the bog. It had to be buried properly, in Old Scratch Wood, where we found it. It had to be returned to its owner.

I eased the box out of my rucksack, trying not to get mud on it. It seemed to weigh a tonne. With shaky hands I took out the skull. It was heavy and dark and strangely hot, almost burning my fingers.

I found myself wondering if it might be able to summon other curlews – or other creatures. I laid it back in the box fast. The problem was, now that I'd seen it again, I didn't want to abandon it. It was almost as if it was part of me – I couldn't bear to lose it. I put the box in my pack and zipped it up tight.

But it kept on calling to me. I could barely remember now why I'd set out across the moor in the first place. All I could think of was the skull. Matt was the one who'd wanted to dump it, not me, I thought. But then he was the reason everything had gone wrong in the first place. Why should I listen to him when he couldn't care less about what happened to my family? There was no need to give it back after all – that wouldn't change anything for Kits. It was stupid to hope. I might as well keep it. No one was going to have it. It was mine.

Then I heard a high keening in the air, far away, sharp and insistent, filling the sky. Louder and louder. My hands were at my ears, pressing hard, desperately trying to keep it away.

The sound swelled and jabbered and screeched. Closer now, almost above me. And it was changing, the blasts lengthening out into a kind of baying cry. Full cry, just like Matt had said. I knew it was coming. My eyes were screwed shut but I could see the pack of creatures making for me, wild and totally pitiless. I could imagine their drool, their stinking breath, the unavoidable slicing teeth. They wouldn't stop until they'd made their kill.

I curled myself into a ball and thought of Kitty lying pale and still and sick, and I tensed every muscle for the killer leap. I could hear them calling for me. *Tilda*, they bayed. *Tilda, Tilda, Tilda.*

'Tilda!'

I jerked up and opened my eyes. The fog swirled close in to the base of the stones where I was huddling. Then I was up and shouting.

'Matt! Over here! Over by the wall!'

There was a stamping and scuffling. Then Matt

loomed out of the fog towards me. Jez leapt forward and into my arms, trying to lick me to death. I don't think I've ever been so happy to see anyone in my whole life.

Matt just stared at me like I was a ghost.

'You've heard it, haven't you?' he said.

I nodded wordlessly.

He suddenly switched into action.

'Drink this,' he said, thrusting a beaker of tea into my hand. It was hot and sweet and soothing. I could feel the sugar pouring into my bloodstream. He wrapped a blanket round me and handed me a slab of veal and ham pie, a flapjack and another cup of tea. I ate mechanically, then realised just how hungry I was. When everything was gone I looked up. I felt like myself again.

'Do you still have the skull?' said Matt. The question broke through my new-found warmth like an ice pick.

'I was going to get rid of it.' I could hear my voice sounding all high-pitched and defensive.

Matt raised his eyebrows. But he hadn't been out here on his own, had he? He wouldn't have lasted a minute in the fog without Jez to guide him. And I bet that when it came down to it, he wouldn't have been able to part with the skull, either.

Matt must have read my mind. He threw me a scorching glance. 'Give it to me then,' he said. 'I'll do it.'

I put a hand to my rucksack and stepped backwards. Matt made a move as if to grab it. I yelled and pushed his hand away.

Suddenly Matt's body slumped. 'We're at it again,' he said. 'We've got to stop. This is exactly what it wants – Alba says it thrives on bad blood.'

We both fell silent and dropped our eyes.

'I'll go into Old Scratch Wood with the skull,' said Matt. 'It's up to me – I'm the one who saw the gabbleratchet. I'm the one who started all this.'

'But Kitty's my sister!' I said, suddenly furious. 'I found it first. I should be the one to take it back.'

Matt shrugged. 'We'll go together, then, if that's what you want,' he said. 'We'll be OK with Jez, won't we?'

I tried to sound confident. ''Course we will,' I said.

'And . . .' He hesitated. 'And Alba says we have to let go of the anger.'

I pictured her knowing grey eyes. Somehow I found myself thinking of the farm and Mum, and my fury at Matt and Aunty Caroline. It didn't seem so important now. What mattered was Kitty. My jaw relaxed, and I nodded.

'You need to do it too,' I said.

I could see Matt was struggling. Thinking of his mum and Paul, I reckoned. His eyebrows came together in a frown. Then he shook himself like a dog coming out of water, and slowly his brow cleared. He looked strong and determined.

'Yeah, OK,' he said. 'I know what you mean. I've got to stop blaming them.'

'Good. Then we're ready as we'll ever be.'

27

Matt

It's impossible to talk in the fog. You just spend all your time looking at the metre or so you can see ahead of you and trying to avoid twisting your ankle on some stray boulder. Jez was at the front with Tilda holding on to her lead, and me at the back. We were all marching on in silence like a crack commando troop sneaking up behind enemy lines.

I didn't want to let my mind dwell on Old Scratch Wood. Instead I kept thinking about my family. It was because of Alba, with her strange way of looking at you and her talk of bad blood. I couldn't help wondering if maybe I'd been too hard on Mum recently.

Don't get me wrong, I love my dad. But he wasn't

always that easy to live with. And if I'm totally honest, he probably wasn't good for her. He was forever going away sailing and never remembering her birthdays or anything. She'd pretty much been on her own for years. I suppose she deserved a bit of company. And Paul makes her happy, even if he is totally boring. I should give him a chance.

Then I remembered that in my dream I'd offered him up to the gabbleratchet without worrying over much about it. I could feel a blush spread across my face, and was glad no one could see me in the fog. I concentrated hard on my feet, keeping in step with Tilda. She had my stick now, and the thuds she was making as she felt for the edge of the path beat a comforting rhythm.

It was easy to forget what we were doing here. My brain just focused on the effort of finding our way through the fog, so that nothing else mattered. But every so often, a picture of Kitty flashed into my mind, wan and tiny, her red-gold hair stuck to her head with sweat. The bargain I thought I'd made had backfired badly. But we were going to change all that. We were going to stop anything from happening to Kitty. We *had* to.

It felt like the fog was thinning just a bit. Wraiths of

mist were curdling round the gorse and rising slowly upwards. It was weird. But yes, it was definitely lifting. As we walked on, the fog rose higher and thinner in the air, and slowly the valley stretched itself out around us. At its bottom we could hear the stream racing.

At last we reached the flat plain that approached the wood. I remembered this bit from before. It was easy going here – a clear path with no boulders or ups and downs. Just low-cropped grass, sheep droppings and the occasional muddy puddle. Then Old Scratch Wood came into blurry view, clinging to the side of the valley in its purple-grey haze.

From being half asleep, I suddenly clicked into red alert. This was it.

We filed along the narrow footpath in silence. As the wood took shape, my skin started to prickle. I hated those runty, twisted trees. *Keep your primeval forest*, I thought. *I'll take a nice bright meadow any day. Or a dusty old London street. Or a run-down estate with drug dealers on every corner, for that matter.* The whole wood was malevolent, crouching in wait for its prey like some repulsive flesh-eating plant.

Tilda seemed to have recovered her energy all of a sudden. Now she looked almost eager.

'Come on, then,' she said.

She set off at top speed with Jez, and after a minute I dragged my feet after her.

I didn't want to go in again. The first time had been bad enough, but my nightmare had made it so much worse. Even though it was cold, I was sweating hard. Just what was I dragging us into?

All I knew was that Kitty was really sick and we had to try and help her, whatever it took.

Now the fog had gone, the wind seemed to be getting up. The trees were waving about big-time, whispering among themselves. Just what we needed. I remembered what Uncle Jack had said about stormy nights, and shivered.

I wasn't on my own this time, though, thank God. Tilda marched straight in, her hand on Jez's neck. I wouldn't have realised that she was frightened at all except that she was breathing too fast. She wasn't like any girl I'd ever known – there was none of that 'I'm so scared' stuff, she just got on with it. It was pretty impressive, though I wasn't so stupid as to tell her that.

The path wasn't wide enough for both of us, so I just followed on, hoping for the best. As we got deeper, the stunted trees seemed to crowd closer together, forming a kind of tunnel. They were even worse than I remembered – dark and dripping with creepy green ferns. They draped over us, stroking our faces with their horrible hairy limbs. Even Tilda was beginning to falter. She turned to look at me, her face shining pale in the darkness of the shade.

'I don't think they want to let us through,' she whispered.

Around us branches rustled and swayed. They were definitely getting closer.

'No. But we've got to try.'

She nodded. I squeezed on to the path beside her and surprised myself by taking her hand. Silently, she gripped mine. We were in this together.

We set off again, ducking to get through the lowest branches and pushing past the twigs that clawed at our arms and legs. Maybe it was just the wind getting stronger, but it didn't seem like that. I could feel fingers running through my hair and kept trying to brush off invisible crawling things. Beside me, Tilda was doing the same. I could hear her panting. Jez whined and kept her head down low. She was clearly hating it.

Ahead I could see a light at the end of the path. *It's got to be the clearing*, I thought. I nudged Tilda. She'd seen it too, and we both started walking faster. Then faster still, trying to keep our cool, trying not to break into a run. Only it wasn't getting any nearer. If anything, the patch of light was shrinking, disappearing into a tiny circle. The trees must be tightening around it. I could feel them pressing in on us. In a minute or two we'd be in the dark.

'Come on!' I hissed in Tilda's ear. 'Quick!'

We abandoned caution and charged ahead, me in front this time, our feet pounding on the leaf-mould path, ignoring the twiggy fingers that reached out to us. Behind us something was whispering and sighing. Adrenalin flooded my limbs. I could hear Tilda right behind me and prayed she would keep up. The end of the tunnel was almost gone.

Suddenly we were scrambling through a dense layer of ferns towards the light. My heart was thumping as if it wanted to get out of my chest, but I kept on surging forwards, desperate not to be left in the darkness.

All at once I fell into the clearing. In a second Tilda was there, too, blinking at the weak sunshine. Finally Jez tore through and just about knocked me over. Above us rose the standing stone – vast, impassive, ancient. We were there.

As my heartbeat slowed, the connection I'd felt with Tilda back on the path dissolved and I remembered her nasty little trick from before with that stupid mask. I got up quickly, glad to have her where I could keep my eyes on her this time. She looked like she'd been dragged through a hedge backwards, which to be fair I suppose she had.

'I should be the one to bury the skull,' said Tilda. 'I dug it up, I should bury it.' She stared at me defiantly. Clearly she wasn't feeling too friendly towards me, either. I didn't attempt to point out that her memory was playing tricks on her. It was me who'd dug the skull up – she'd just stood there and watched.

'Yeah, OK, whatever,' I said. 'But it should be in the same place. By the standing stone.'

Tilda hesitated. For once she seemed nervous. Then she walked slowly over to the stone, knelt down and started to dig away at the earth around it. Nothing looked disturbed, but the soil gave way easily enough. She started excavating in earnest, and soon her fingers were covered with dark rich humus.

I was itching to get on with it myself. She was taking so long. I just hoped she'd have the guts to drop the skull in there once she'd dug the hole.

The wind was higher now and the stunted trees creaked and whined. They seemed to have huddled even closer together, so that less and less light trickled through. I glanced round at them, then came and knelt beside Tilda. I didn't want her distracted, but it felt like a good idea to get the whole thing over and done with as quickly as possible.

Tilda didn't look up. Her eyes had gone glazed and distant, and her hands scrabbled away at the earth. In a sort of trance she reached inside her rucksack for the box and took out the skull.

There was a whirring overhead. I peered up to a dwindling fragment of sky. Way off in the air I could see a V shape. A skein of geese, their shapes just coming into focus.

Tilda stopped. She stared at the ground, holding the skull, like a zombie in some rubbish movie.

'Go on,' I hissed. 'Drop it in.'

Tilda's lips twisted into a snarl that totally shocked me. Suddenly she looked terrifying.

I made a swift decision. I grabbed at the skull and prised her fingers away from it. Tilda gripped harder, and all of a sudden the paper-thin cranium caved in with a sharp crack and broke away in fragments.

We both gazed down at it in horror. The curved beak was still in Tilda's hand attached to the jagged remains of the head. The skull's beauty was gone – it just looked evil now.

There was no time to think. I made a grab for the

beak and threw it into the hole. Then I caught hold of one of Tilda's hands and dragged her to her feet.

'Come on,' I shouted. 'We're getting out of here.'

Tilda seemed to sway. Her pupils widened and she came to.

'You're right,' she said in a tiny voice. 'I've got to let it go.'

I tugged her arm. Way up in the sky the whistling had started. 'Come on,' I yelled. 'Tilda!'

She jerked to attention. 'Wait,' she said. She shook off my hand and dropped down on her knees. I hoped to God she wouldn't touch the skull again. Every nerve in my body was telling me to run, but somehow I made myself stay.

Tilda picked up a handful of earth and flung it on to the remains. Then another, and another, until at last the vile thing was gone.

'It's all yours,' she yelled in a shaky voice. 'So leave us alone.' She scrambled to her feet.

Perhaps it would be enough.

Then we were legging it through the clearing and along the path and through the crowding twisted trees, back towards the daylight.

28

Tilda

I kept up with Matt, but only just. I truly thought my chest was going to explode. Jez lunged ahead, picking out a route I'd never taken before. There was no path – just piles of boulders everywhere, and great lumps of moss and ledges dripping with ferns and branches so low we both had to run in a kind of crouch, and even then we kept having to swerve to avoid them. If we didn't stop soon, I was going to be sick.

At last light filtered in through the trees. We were at the edge of the wood. Now all I could hear was the sound of the stream and my rasping breath. We'd made it. And I'd managed to let go of the skull, even though I'd so desperately wanted to keep hold of it. I didn't know what had happened to me at the standing stone, but that thing was finally back where it belonged. It couldn't touch me any more. I felt giddy with relief.

As if reading my thoughts, Matt turned to me.

'We've done it!' he said. 'It's over.' He looked jubilant. 'Look. The fog's completely gone. We've got out. We're going to be all right.'

'Do you think so?' I was still shaking. I couldn't quite believe it yet.

'Yes. I really do. What matters is that we've got rid of the skull. That's what was making all those things happen. But it's over now – it must be. Gabe told me—' He stopped suddenly.

'What? What did he tell you?'

Matt hesitated.

'He said that both our mums had something to do with the curlew skull when they were young.'

I knew it. I just knew it. What had Gabe said?

Matt rubbed his face. 'I'll tell you all about it, but not now,' he said. 'We've got to get back before dark.'

He called to Jez and started rapidly down the hill out of the wood.

I didn't have the energy to push for more details. I

was unbelievably tired, tireder than the tiredest thing on earth. It felt as though a year of lie-ins wouldn't be enough. I'd have been happy to curl up on the open moor and go to sleep there and then if Matt would have let me.

Then I remembered Kitty. Only the thought of her could spur me on now. If we got back safely, would there be good news about her? She had to get well. I couldn't bear to think about the alternative. I hurried to catch up, and my breath came in little short gasps.

'Do you feel any different?' Matt said as I came level with him.

'How do you mean?'

'Well . . . you've been acting sort of weird about the skull. I wondered if getting rid of it had made you . . . well . . . feel better?'

He was right. I didn't have to think about the skull any more. The further I got away from it, the lighter I felt. I glanced sideways at Matt. He was walking a bit taller, a bit straighter, kind of purposeful-looking. Perhaps I'd not been seeing him properly before.

I didn't know if that was the skull's influence, or something deeper inside me, like a long grief that was at last beginning to fade. Whatever it was, all the bitterness that had been eating away at me had vanished, leaving me just really, really exhausted. I wanted an end to all the fighting and sniping and hating. Suddenly I was embarrassed at the way I'd behaved since Matt had arrived. It had been truly awful. I wondered if there was more to it than I'd realised. Was it possible that I'd been jealous of Matt still having his mother when I'd lost mine? Whatever it was, I needed to get over it.

And maybe, when we got back and everything was all right, Matt and I could have a go at being friends.

If we ever got home, that was. My bones seemed to have turned into lead. The fog had disappeared without a trace, but the sky was clouding over fast, making it seem dark even though dusk was a fair way off. It was cold now and the wind was whipping round in big gusts that made you take a step or two backwards if they hit you full on. It felt like a storm was brewing. But at least I had Matt and Jez this time. It made all the difference in the world.

I'd blanked out those awful hours beside the wall on my own in the horrible grey fog, but it was all coming back to me now. Those terrifying creatures I'd heard – had they just been inside my head? They'd disappeared when Matt and Jez arrived, so I supposed they must have been.

Did that mean that everything Gabe had warned us about was a load of old rubbish, too? The skull, the omens, the gabbleratchet – everything? I was beginning to wonder. I mean, all that stuff with the crow on the roof was pure mumbo-jumbo. Maybe a bit too much of that had rubbed off on Alba as well.

Yes, we'd definitely done way too much listening to stupid stories. And now we'd spooked ourselves silly over the skull in Old Scratch Wood. What a pair of idiots.

I touched Matt's arm.

'Do you think Kitty's going to be all right?' I said.

'I was just thinking about that,' he said. 'I really hope so.'

'Maybe it was just a virus and she's sitting up in bed now stuffing herself with chocolate.'

He smiled. 'Maybe. So get a move on and let's get out of this and find out.'

Matt had a point. The wind was getting wilder and wilder. Jez pulled on her lead and whined as if to warn me to hurry up. Normally I'd let her run free, but I didn't want to risk her running off today of all days, and I was so tired that I was quite happy for her to drag me along behind her. At least the going was much faster than it had been in the fog. We'd already reached the dry stone wall and turned towards the tor. It wouldn't be long now.

'So what exactly was Gabe saying about Mum and Aunty Rose?' I asked Matt.

He carried on walking for a few steps and I wondered if he'd heard. Then he turned and faced me.

'He said your mum had a curlew – a live one, only it was hurt. But it died – Gabe . . . killed it. My mum asked him to. And she buried it in Old Scratch Wood.'

I gasped. How was that possible? Then I thought of the velvet the skull had been lying on – the material of Aunty Caroline's dress – and knew it had to be true.

Matt related the story Gabe had told him. I listened, but it didn't make much sense to me.

'So Gabe and Aunty Caroline went back to Old Scratch Wood and hid the skull?' I said. 'And Mum just forgot about it? I don't get it. How come I found it again, then? I think Gabe's making up all the gabbleratchet stuff just to scare us.'

Matt said nothing. And suddenly I knew there was more.

'Tell me,' I said. And so, in fits and starts, he told me.

I couldn't believe what he was saying. That phone

call I'd overheard when Aunty Caroline was fighting with Mum. She'd told Mum where the skull was hidden. Sent her running to Old Scratch Wood. Signed her death warrant.

The wind buffeted my ears, but I scarcely felt it any more.

'You mean your mum was responsible for the accident?' I said. I was trembling with anger.

Matt shook his head, but his voice faltered.

'She didn't know what would happen. Maybe your mum made her tell – I don't know. Anyway, it wasn't Mum's fault, what came afterwards. And the accident might just have been a coincidence.'

The wind was howling around us. It sounded almost like an animal. A pack of dogs or something.

'You think so?' I said. I was walking so fast I nearly tripped over Jez. 'Then you're a complete jerk.' I rubbed the tears from my eyes. 'Aunty Caroline might as well have run over Mum herself.'

Matt looked away. He didn't try to argue, which was a good thing because I don't know what I'd have said to him if he had. I marched on ahead of him, and every time he came near I sped up. Rage was giving me new strength. My mind seethed with images of Mum and the skull, Mum and Kitty, Mum being lowered into the cold hard ground.

The howling was louder. I could swear it was real. I glanced behind me, suddenly nervous. But it was nothing. Nothing but the wind. I started walking faster.

At last we reached the farm gate. Perhaps Dad really would be back by now, wondering where we were. Kitty might actually be waiting for us, looking out for us. Maybe, just maybe, everything was going to be all right. My whole skin tingled with hope as we reached the porch of the house. I leant over to put my key in the door. Then I froze.

'Matt,' I whispered. 'Look.'

Above our heads, dangling from the porch roof by a string, was a strange object. We craned our necks upwards. It twirled slowly in the breeze, its empty eyes staring straight at us.

The skull.

Only it wasn't a bird any more.

29

Matt

I pushed Tilda and Jez out of the porch, away from the thing that was hanging there.

'Uncle Jack!' I yelled. 'Kitty!'

There was no sound. Uncle Jack's car wasn't there – he must still be at the hospital. I turned back to the porch again. The skull was dangling there, dark and vicious and unexplainable, swinging in the wind. I wanted to pull it down and stamp on it, destroy it for ever.

With an effort, I tore my eyes away. Tilda's mouth had gone slack. Her red hair seemed very bright against her face.

'But the skull was all smashed up,' she said.

'I know. And in the ground.'

'It can't be the same one.'

'It isn't,' I said. 'Look at it. It's much bigger. And it doesn't have a beak. It's got teeth. Fangs. It's more like a dog or something, I don't know what. Somebody must be having a joke. A really terrible joke.' I tried to smile, but I shouldn't think it came out very well. My spine felt as if tarantulas were crawling up and down it.

Tilda nodded slowly. 'I suppose so,' she said. 'It's Hallowe'en after all. Maybe that's it. But it still feels like our skull, all the same.'

I knew what she meant. Once again we both stared up. It was beginning to get dark. The wind grabbed Tilda's hair and blew it across her face.

Neither of us wanted to go into the house with that thing hanging there.

'Let's put the chickens away,' said Tilda. Her voice sounded shaky.

Together we went through to the back yard. The geese must have heard us, because they started hissing and honking, then came racing towards us from the little side yard, holding their necks out straight ahead of them. I tried not to look worried. Someone must have left the gate open. I hoped it wasn't me.

Behind the tor, the moon was beginning to come up low on the horizon, huge and silver and entirely full. You could almost see it move.

Jez shifted and whined. Suddenly the geese flapped their wings in unison, ran forward and took off into the sky. We stared at them transfixed. I felt Tilda edge closer to me.

'We clipped their wings,' she whispered. 'They never fly.'

I gazed after the geese, too shocked to say anything. From the direction of the tor came the long high quaver of a horn, then three blasts in quick succession. In the distance I could hear a kind of howling. Though the light was fading, I thought I could make out the black outlines of creatures streaming down from the tor towards the farm. What were they? They looked a bit like dogs. This was all too weird. I wondered if we should be running.

Tilda gazed at the creatures and let out a breath.

'Wow,' she said. 'It's the Hunt. How amazing. The hounds must have picked up a scent. We don't normally see them over here.' She hesitated. 'But this is really late for them to be out. I thought they only hunted in the mornings.'

I was pulling at her hand, but she wriggled free.

'Look at them,' she said. 'They're just foxhounds, Matt. There's nothing to be scared of.'

I peered at the hounds racing towards us. A couple of them had reached the boundary of the farm and were running up and down outside the dry stone wall, then they scrambled up it and stood on the top, eyeing us. They looked strangely familiar.

'Lightfoot!' Tilda yelled. 'Lawless!'

I didn't know how she could tell at this distance, but I guessed she was right. My chest loosened a little.

'They must have got out and met up with the Hunt somehow,' Tilda said. 'But they shouldn't be hunting with the pack – they haven't been trained properly yet. I can't see any riders, though. Maybe the rest of the hounds escaped from the Hunt kennels and Lightfoot and Lawless joined up with them. I'd better phone the kennel man and tell him.' She made a move towards the two hounds.

'Don't,' I said, and grabbed her hand.

Tilda was right – it was the overgrown puppies. But something about their eyes had changed. They were sort of hard and blank, and they were staring straight at us. One of them – Lightfoot? Lawless? I didn't know – bared his teeth and let out a long, low growl. Tilda took a step back. Behind the puppies were other hounds, bigger ones, leaping for the wall. They'd clear it easily.

We looked at each other. Then we turned and fled.

I snatched a glance behind us as we pounded away. Lightfoot and Lawless were already racing through the field towards the farmhouse. We were nearly in the front yard, but I knew the front door was still locked. We wouldn't make it in time.

'East Barn,' I yelled.

The pack was in the vegetable garden now. The noise of their yipping and baying rose behind us, but we didn't stop. I pelted round the corner into the front yard and dived into the barn. Tilda and Jez shot in behind me. The hounds were bearing down and the yard filled with their cries, a cacophony of screeching, yowling, yapping barks. My worst nightmare – but this time I wasn't sleeping.

The gabbleratchet was here. It wasn't a dream – there was no doubt about it. It was a hunt. And we were the quarry.

Just in time I slammed the door and wrenched down the wooden latch to secure it. The hounds flung themselves against it, testing it. It wouldn't stand up to them for long.

30

Tilda

My mind was gibbering with shock. I reached for Jez, who was trembling even more than I was. Matt was pacing up and down in the darkness of the barn. Gabe must have moved the cow and its calf back to the fields yesterday, but it still smelt pleasantly of hay and dung. Only now we were trapped.

Outside the demented barking was getting more and more frenzied, and the door groaned with the slam of bodies against it. *Thump*, it went. *Thump*.

I breathed out, expelling all the air right down to my stomach, then again and again. It worked – I didn't feel quite so faint any more. But the hounds weren't giving up.

Thump.

'They definitely must have escaped from the Hunt kennels,' I said. 'I bet the kennel man will be round soon. He'll take them home.'

Matt gave a choked laugh. He was standing below the little window at the back of the barn, and his face was lit up by the horrible sun-like moon.

'You saw how the skull had changed, didn't you?' he said.

Suddenly I could see it in every detail as it twirled in the breeze. The broad head, the long flattish muzzle. The teeth. It had been the skull of a hound.

'First geese, then hounds,' I whispered.

'We should have known,' said Matt. 'I knew the gabbleratchet was hellhounds. I just didn't think they'd be real.'

The barn door shook and groaned. Through a thin crack I could see that the front yard was full of dark shapes, all legs and mouths and eyes and that hideous baying cry. I shut my eyes, but it just made the noise more frightening, so I forced them open again.

'We've got to get out of here,' said Matt. 'That door's going to give way soon.'

Thump.

239

He spun round. 'That little window at the back,' he said. 'We might just be able to get through it.'

He grabbed a straw bale and dumped it under the window, then ran for another one. I shook myself and joined him in making a pile.

'You go first,' said Matt. 'I'll help you up.'

The idea of going outside terrified me. What if the hounds realised what we were up to? What if they got hold of our scent and found their way round to the back of the barn? But staying here wasn't an option. The door sounded as if it was about to splinter.

'What about Jez?' I said.

'She'll have to manage on her own.'

I turned and faced him. 'She's coming with us.'

Matt's mouth twisted, but he knew I wouldn't give in. He let out a sharp breath. 'OK, we'll have a go. If you get through first, I'll try and pass her up to the window. Maybe you can pull her out. But be quick.'

He gave me a leg up. The window was tight, but I managed to haul myself through. I thanked my lucky stars that East Barn backs on to the side yard, which is entirely enclosed except for the gate leading round to the other side. I'd be safe here for a moment or two.

It was a big drop down, though. I breathed in, shut my eyes and jumped. At the front of the barn the crazed baying continued unbroken.

I looked back up again. Jez's paws appeared at the window then disappeared. I held my breath. At last they reappeared again.

'Come on, girl,' I whispered. 'Come on.' And suddenly she was twisting through and balancing on the sill and springing down to me, and I was holding my hand over her muzzle to stop her from barking, and hugging her tight.

My heart was racing so hard I thought I might collapse. I was desperate to run now, but I forced myself to wait till Matt appeared. As I cast my eyes around in panic, I spotted something against the back wall of East Barn that that might just help us. Gabe must have left it there by mistake. I offered a silent prayer of thanks.

'Come on, Matt,' I said under my breath.

There was a violent splintering of wood and an eruption of baying. The hounds must be nearly inside the barn.

Then Matt was down on the ground beside me, panting as if he'd never stop. I let go of Jez and grabbed hold of his hand.

'I only just did it,' he said. 'I didn't think I'd make it in time.' His eyes were wide and starey.

'If we're really quiet we can sneak through to the back yard from here while they're still in the front one, then into the vegetable garden,' I whispered. 'They might not see us. With luck we'll be able to get into the house through the back door. If it's open, that is.'

He shook his head. 'They'll catch us. They'll trace our scent to the window and work it out. They're going to hunt us, Tilda. To the death.'

Suddenly I felt furious. We couldn't give in. The gabbleratchet wasn't going to defeat us. There had to be a way to stop this.

'Not if I can help it,' I said.

I picked up the petrol can I'd found by the wall and unscrewed the lid. Then I fished in my coat pocket and waved a box of matches in the air.

'Take these,' I said. 'I'll lay a trail of petrol. If they start following, you've got to light it straight away. Now come on, and be careful not to step in it. If you don't want to fry, that is.'

I stole away, one hand on Jez's collar, the other clutching the petrol can. Matt was standing in a kind of daze, still too shocked to move. But at last he pulled himself together and followed me.

Cautiously we skirted round the back of East Barn. We could hear the hounds inside the barn now, looking for us. There was no time to hang about. I glanced at Matt and he nodded. I stepped well away from the wall and started pouring a line of petrol on to the flagstones.

Suddenly the noise changed. There was a flurry of yaps and a deep, low growling. I turned round and felt my gaze being drawn upwards.

There on the windowsill, staring down at us, was Lawless. I don't know how he'd managed to get up there on his own, but he had. His eyes met mine. There was nothing in them that I recognised any more.

He sniffed the air. Then he raised his head and howled.

31

Matt

We started running. Already we were out of the side yard and crossing the back yard past the chicken shed towards the back garden, and Tilda kept on sloshing out petrol behind her like there was no tomorrow. In shaking fingers I held a match ready.

And all at once the hounds were surging out of the front yard and through towards us in a black river, and Jez was growling back at them and trying to shake off Tilda's hand.

'Now!' she screamed.

I lit the match and threw.

The flames shot up. One of the hounds fell and

yelped in pain. The rest wheeled round in a mass of dark bodies, snarling and snapping. One started to howl. Was it Lawless? Then the others took up the call. The cry of the gabbleratchet rose again, cold and deathly and utterly terrifying.

We raced towards the back door.

Please, please don't let it be locked, I prayed.

I got there first and turned the knob. Miraculously, wonderfully, utterly fantastically, the door opened. Tilda dragged Jez through and we banged it shut and bolted it top and bottom.

I hurtled through the hall and bolted the front door, too. Tilda was clinging to Jez as if she'd never let her go.

'Let's take her upstairs,' she said. 'I don't want her near them.'

We bundled Jez up and into Tilda's room. Tilda slumped on to her bed and Jez got up with her. I swept a load of untidy clothes off a chair and fell into it.

'Maybe they'll give up now,' said Tilda. But she didn't sound like she believed it for a moment.

I wanted to play along, but I couldn't. Outside the hounds were swarming round the back door, baying for our blood.

'Listen,' I said. 'They're not going to give up.'

'Why?' said Tilda. 'How do you know?' I could hear the beginning of a wail catch at the back of her words.

'I don't know. But I can feel it in my bones. It's him. Old Scratch. The devil. First he wanted Kitty. And now he wants me, too.'

Outside the clamour of the hounds had moved closer. It sounded as if it was right under the bedroom window. Suddenly we heard the smashing of glass and the baying grew higher and higher. They were inside the house.

We both froze. Then together we began pushing the chest of drawers against the door.

Tilda sat on her bed and hugged Jez close. We waited. And waited.

I knew it was all because of me. I'd made that stupid bargain in my dream. I'd told myself that sacrificing Paul was the only thing I could do. But I'd wanted it, too. I'd wanted him out of the picture, out of my life, even though I knew Mum loved him. Knew that she wanted to marry him. And now Kitty would die – and me and maybe Tilda too.

I crept over to the window, keeping my head down. The frenzied barking was louder still, and down below I could hear baying and crashing. It wouldn't take them long to find us.

Suddenly I realised what I had to do. My stomach churned as I peeked down at the creatures swarming beneath the window. But I had to save Tilda – whatever it took.

I unfastened the latch and pushed the window ajar. The sound of the hounds rose louder.

'Matt!' said Tilda. She sounded terrified. 'What are you doing?'

I looked back at her.

'I'm going down there. I'll draw them away from here. Maybe I can trap them in a barn and get help. I've got to do *something*!'

I put my hands to the frame and started lifting myself up.

'No!' Tilda whispered urgently. 'You'll get yourself killed!'

'I have to,' I said. 'Don't worry. I'll be really careful. It'll mean you'll have a chance. And Kitty, too. And it's all my fault anyway.'

All at once I was being dragged back to the floor.

'Don't!' Tilda yelled. Her words rushed out helter-skelter. 'Matt, it's not your fault.' She took a breath. 'And it's not Aunty Caroline's, either. I . . . I know Mum wasn't very fair to her. I heard her once on the phone to your mum, and Dad tried to tell her she wasn't being very reasonable about the fields, but she wouldn't listen. And then after Mum died Aunty Caroline wrote me a letter trying to explain everything. But . . . I threw it away.'

I had clenched my fists. With an effort I unclenched them again. Slowly I took Tilda's hand, and at once she seemed to gather her strength. She looked fierce and proud and unbeaten.

'I love this place,' she said. 'But you're my cousin. My family. Whatever happens with the farm, we'll deal with it. It doesn't matter. We've got to stop all this. I won't let everything be poisoned any more.'

She stopped abruptly.

'Matt,' she said in a trembling voice. 'I can smell burning.'

I peered out of the window. A wisp of smoke rose upwards, filling my nostrils and making my eyes water. The living room must be on fire. I didn't know how it had happened – maybe one of the hounds had sparks in its fur when it broke in. Maybe the gabble-ratchet just destroyed everything in its path. I'd no idea. But we couldn't stay here. We'd be burned alive.

'Quick! Help me move the chest of drawers again,' I said. 'We've got to get out.'

Behind us, something growled – a low, hostile

growl that made my skin go cold. We both swung round.

Jez was standing in front of the chest. There were flecks of foam at the side of her mouth and her eyes were rolling. For a moment I couldn't work out what was going on. Then Tilda seemed to take it in. She made a lunge towards Jez, but I grabbed her and pulled her back and held her there.

Everything was in slow motion. I could hear my heart beating, and Tilda's rapid shallow breathing. Jez's body was twisting and writhing, her eyes fixed on Tilda's in what looked like longing.

As we watched, she seemed to grow, bigger and bigger, her delicate features blunting into something coarse and vicious. Her eyes turned from caramel to a blank cold stare. Then she was on her feet again, huge and tall and menacing. She snarled and bared her teeth at me.

We were lost.

'The window!' Tilda yelled.

I pulled her arm. 'You go,' I said. 'I'll try and keep her off.'

'No! She won't hurt me. She loves me. Just go!'

There was no time to argue. I did what she said, not letting my eyes off Jez as I stepped into the frame. In the light of the flames I could see two huge hounds down on the path below. They craned their necks up and howled. I could hear more on the stairs, barking and baying. In a minute they would be here.

I cast about desperately for a hold. There was ivy everywhere, but I didn't dare trust it. At last I grabbed onto a drainpipe and levered myself out. Smoke filled my eyes and lungs, and I coughed and heaved. But it had to be possible. There was a narrow ridge all round the house that looked as if it might be strong enough to carry our weight. If we were very, very careful, we could make it to the front – away from the hounds.

Jez let out a low snarl. I turned back and peered into the room. She was inching towards Tilda. Nearer and nearer. Drool dripped from her mouth.

'Sit, Jez,' Tilda was saying. Her voice was trembling. 'Good girl. Sit. Jezebel, sit!'

'Get a move on, Tilda,' I said. 'Now!'

Tilda pulled herself out beside me. Her face was a mess of tears and she was spluttering in the smoke. I stared back inside, unable to tear my eyes away. Jez growled again, a deep rasp that made her whole body shake. We edged back along the ridge, clinging to the ivy, hoping to goodness it would hold.

Suddenly Jez tensed all her muscles. She snarled

again. And then she sprang towards us through the open window. I saw her claws scrabble desperately on the slate tiles, failing to find a purchase.

And then she hurtled through the air and fell to the ground.

The last thing I heard was Tilda's scream.

32

rilda

I don't know if I understand everything now, or if I ever will. Matt says that when we got down off the roof I passed out. I do remember the hounds going quiet though, just after Jez fell. According to Matt, Gabe and the kennel man came and rounded them up, only by then there wasn't anything strange about them at all. And I remember Alba stroking my forehead down in our kitchen after Gabe had put out the fire. But she's saying nothing.

In front of me the sea was grey and the sky was grey and so was everything between. There's no black and white. Everything merges, everything fades into everything else. In art class at school they teach us not to draw the edges. To look at how the light slips over solid forms and liquefies them. Who knows what's solid anyway?

Matt and I walked in silence along the beach. A tangled trail of debris marked the high-water line. It was bladderwrack and torn plastic beakers and the occasional strange object tossed up by the sea. A single trainer. A tiny bleached crab, belly up, its limbs hugging salt air. When I stood on a clump of seaweed, flies rose in a black cloud.

Far off down the bay I could see a curlew standing alert, staring out towards the horizon. In my dreams I could still trace the line of its skull and weigh it in the palm of my hand.

I nudged Matt and pointed. 'Curlew,' I said.

He couldn't spot it at first. Then he found it and half smiled. He took a picture of it, checked it had come out OK and passed the camera to me.

'Not a whimbrel, then?' he said, teasing. 'You're positive?'

I shrugged, smiling back. How could I be sure of anything any more? It didn't matter though. We don't need to worry about curlews or geese or anything else. The evil has gone out of them. Gabe says it's gone from Parson's Farm now, and I want to believe him.

Maybe it was never there at all. I just don't know.

We were lucky Gabe came to look for us that night. He'd been out on the moor trying to find us, but then he heard the hounds and came straight here. He says the fire wasn't too bad – it never caught the rest of the house, though it's made a horrible mess of the living room. It looked as if the hounds had already trashed it anyway. Apparently the Hunt staff had been searching for them for hours, all over the moor. They've taken Lightfoot and Lawless to join the pack now, and I'm glad. I don't think I want to see them again.

Matt ambled off down to the edge of the sea and started skimming stones into it. I watched him select them carefully, then throw a five straight off. He's good at a lot of things, though I didn't used to think so. He seems to be getting back to normal, too. Yesterday he was totally drained, as if the whole experience had sapped the lifeblood out of him. Today he's acting more like a human being. But I know there are scars you can't see. We both have them.

I went to join Matt at the waterline. Together we scanned the horizon, the waves lapping our boots. Neither of us seemed to want to talk. It was enough to stare out to sea. But it didn't last long. From high up on the beach there was a cry.

'Matt! Tilda! Wait for me!'

In a tumble of arms and legs, Kitty dashed across the sand towards us. Behind her was Dad, striding down to us and laughing. He caught up with Kitty, grabbed her and swung her round.

'So much for keeping this one in the car so she doesn't get cold,' he said. 'She's not having any of it.'

Kitty giggled as he put her down. 'I'm all better now,' she said 'Look.' She did a wobbly pirouette, then raced along the beach, her hair a fluffy cloud of red-gold.

Dad rolled his eyes. 'Unbelievable,' he said. 'Only two days ago she was at death's door. And now . . . I don't know where she gets the energy.'

Matt and I exchanged glances. We'd not told him everything. There didn't seem any point. We weren't going to start bringing up the gabbleratchet now. And to be honest, I think we were both more than happy to forget it.

Aunty Caroline waved from the edge of the beach, and I waved back to her. I know that she and Dad talked about the farm when she came down here last night, and they're going to sort something out together. The farm won't need to be sold after all. And this morning Aunty Caroline went to see Mum's grave, just her on her own, and when she came back I could see she'd been crying.

She's taking Matt to London tonight. He's going to stay with her and Paul, though his dad arrives back from his sailing trip in a few days, so there'll be an escape route if Matt needs it. But he's promised to come back here in the spring half term. We might go sailing together. And maybe I'll go and visit him in the Christmas holidays. Check out London for a couple of days and see some sights. I suppose it won't kill me to leave the farm for a bit. Perhaps even do some Christmas shopping with Aunty Caroline. Who knows?

Dad got in step with us.

'Look at your sister, Tilda,' he said. 'Isn't it marvellous? But I'm so sorry about Jez, sweetheart. I know you're missing her terribly. I've spoken to the vet and he thinks she must have had some kind of fit, to have jumped like that. Maybe the fire drove her mad. I don't think she suffered, though.'

But I knew that she had.

I blinked back the tears for about the twelfth time today and watched Kitty playing at the edge of the waves. Then I looked up at the blank grey sky.

Way up high I thought I could see something

move. A V shape, incredibly far off. Maybe I was imagining it. But I reckoned it was a skein of geese, arriving from their autumn migration. Thousands and thousands of miles, each taking turns to lead the formation while the others coasted in their slipstream. The same every year, without fail. It's not like that for us. Matt and I don't know what the future's going to bring. Just that there *is* a future, and that Kitty's there to enjoy it, even though my lovely Jez isn't.

I strained my eyes and watched until I was quite sure they were gone. Then I turned to Matt. 'Race you to the curlew,' I said. 'Last one there's a wuss.'

And I ran off in the direction Kitty had taken without once looking behind me.

Acknowledgements

Many thanks to Barry Cunningham, my editor Rachel Leyshon and all at Chicken House for bringing this book into being, and to my agent, Anna Power, for her help and support.

I'm deeply grateful to the Undiscovered Voices 2012 team at the Society of Children's Book Writers and Illustrators for noticing, publicising and anthologising the first two chapters, and to Catherine Johnson, who gave me encouragement and brilliant advice as part of the Apprenticeships in Fiction scheme and beyond. Thanks also for help and advice from AiF director Marion Urch, for comments on early drafts by Chris Waters and Clare Hawkins and for farming wisdom from Ian Forbes and Alan Hill.

And a final thank you to John, who sat through endless re-readings, checked the sails and demanded extra scariness.

THE
SKULL
IN THE
WOOD

sandra greaves

*give your
ears a treat!*

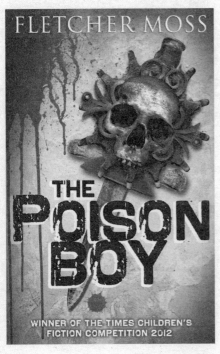